The Norrington Collection

CLEAN REGENCY ROMANCE

THE LADY SERIES
BOOK FOUR

DAISY LANDISH

Copyright © 2024 by Daisy Landish
All rights reserved.

No part of this book may be reproduced in any form or by any electronic or mechanical means, including information storage and retrieval systems, without written permission from the author, except for the use of brief quotations in a book review.

Editing by Jessica McKenna
Cover by Daisy Landish

BEACHES AND TRAILS
PUBLISHING

About Daisy Landish

Daisy Landish is a romance and contemporary fiction author living in the UK, whose clean and sweet novellas have tugged at readers' heartstrings across the pond and beyond. When she's not writing love stories, Daisy spends her time reading, hiking at dawn, and riding into the sunset on her horse, Rosebud.

Join Daisy's Newsletter for updates and giveaways!
www.daisylandishromance.com

- facebook.com/daisylandishromance
- x.com/daisy_landish
- instagram.com/beachesandtrailspublishing
- amazon.com/author/daisylandish
- bookbub.com/authors/daisy-landish
- goodreads.com/Daisy_Landish

Also by Daisy Landish

Clean Regency Romance

The Lady Series - The Allington Collection
The Lady Series - The Gillingham Collection
The Lady Series - The Blackmore Collection
The Lady Series - The Norrington Collection

Clean Contemporary Romance

Love on Spruce Island
Second Chance
Cherry Tree Island
The Wedding Trio
Extra Credit
Counting on the Cowboy
Focusing on the Cowboy
Mistletoe Magic
Grounded at Christmas

Cozy Mysteries

Jane and Kennedy Daniels Mysteries
Pine Grove Mysteries
Annie Archer Paranormal Mysteries
Wilma Wade Holiday Mysteries
Mike and Maddie Mysteries
Mystic Moonhaven Mysteries
Sweater Weather: Cozy Mysteries for Fall
Summer Vibes: Cozy Mysteries for Summer
Let it Snow: Cozy Mysteries for Winter

Discovering The Lady
A CLEAN REGENCY ROMANCE

Chapter One

Humming softly, Lady Charlotte Norrington, the first daughter of the late Duke of Ravenswood, walked down the red-carpeted staircase to the vast foyer. Her mother and brother had summoned her to the drawing room. A smile graced her round face when she heard her younger sisters, Amelia and Sophia, arguing with their French teacher.

Clad in a lavender silk gown, its delicate embroidery accentuating her slender figure, she swept into the drawing room with the grace befitting her station. The room, a tapestry of pastel hues, portraits, and ornaments, spelt of wealth. The flickering candlelight lent a warm glow to the room, casting shadows that danced along the ornate walls. The room exuded an air of regal elegance, a reflection of the Norrington family's standing in Society.

Charlotte curtsied to her mother, the Dowager Duchess, and her older brother, William, the Duke of Ravenswood. Both were impeccably dressed in finery. She sat on the settee beside her mother with the poise expected of a lady.

"Charlotte, my dear," the Dowager Duchess began, her voice somewhat hesitant. "There is a matter of great importance we must discuss."

Charlotte immediately surmised what it would be about. At nine and ten and about to begin her second season, the onus was on her to do well and find a perfect match for a husband. She didn't look forward to attending multiple tedious soirees in the bid to find a worthy suitor. Just as she had in her first season, she wished she could find a man she fancied, who would fall in love with her on the first night of the ball and propose immediately.

The Duke of Ravenswood, a figure of commanding presence with his tall frame, broad shoulders, and round handsome face, fixed his ocean-blue eyes on her identical ones from his position by the fireplace. "Our family's financial standing has become precarious, and we must take decisive action."

Charlotte, maintaining a composed expression, listened intently to the gravity of her family's financial situation, or lack thereof. It appalled her to learn that their father, who died a year ago, had left them in penury because of his love for gambling.

William, with a sombre demeanour, continued, "I've heard whispers that the Duke of Malvern seeks a wife. It would be in the family's best interest for you to consider his suit."

Charlotte gasped. Surely William must be jesting. The Duke of Malvern, a man of mature years and ample wealth, was known for his rather distinguished position. She, however, shuddered at the thought of a union with a man old enough to be her father.

"William, I cannot imagine myself marrying a man so old. Why, he must have children my age from his late wife," she protested, her ocean-blue eyes reflecting her inner turmoil. "Surely there must be an alternative."

Her mother, the epitome of maternal elegance, intervened with a soothing tone. "My dear, we understand your apprehension, but we must consider the future of the family. Marrying the duke would secure our standing and provide financial stability."

"With his business connection, I could salvage our family's dwindled coffers," William added, rubbing his clean-shaven chin.

As both her mother and brother continued trying to convince her to accept their proposal, the weight of duty and societal expectations pressed upon Charlotte. A tension born from the clash between personal desires and familial obligations flooded her. From a young age, she had always wanted to marry for love.

The atmosphere in the drawing room grew fraught as Charlotte kept mute as she comprehended the gravity of her family's financial plight. She dreaded how the season would play out. The competition for the Duke of Malvern's favour would be ruthless because, unlike her, she knew some debutantes would be desperate to have him show interest in them because of his wealth and the coveted title of being a duchess.

"Charlotte," her mother implored, her pleading gaze meeting hers. "We understand the sacrifices we ask of you, but it is for the greater good of the family. The future of the Norringtons depends on your willingness to embrace this duty."

William's brow furrowed with concern as he stared at her. "I have taken measures to secure a substantial dowry for you. The funds I borrowed should make you a highly desirable match in the eyes of the duke."

The news struck Charlotte like a thunderclap. Her brother had sacrificed his own financial security to ensure her success in the matrimonial pursuit? What would he do if she couldn't catch Duke Malvern's fancy? How would he pay back? The weight of duty bore down on her shoulders, threatening to crush the dreams of love and companionship she had always harboured in her heart.

She relayed her fears. "But what if the duke chooses another bride? Surely you must know that other ladies would vie for his attention."

William and their mother shared a look that she didn't understand. Her mother reached out to hold her hand and squeeze it.

William drew abreast to sit on the brocaded armchair beside the French windows.

"We've come up with a plan."

She frowned. "Plan?"

"Yes. Mother will make sure you have him on your dance card, but the rest will be up to you."

Her frown deepened. "What do I do?"

"You're to lead the duke to the garden so that he would be alone with you."

Her ocean-blue eyes widened like saucers. "You want to have us in a compromising situation?"

"It's the only way. Mother and I will come along with the gossips of the *ton* and he will have no choice but to marry you."

Appalled by the lengths her family would go to secure their future, Charlotte excused herself from the drawing room. As she ascended the grand staircase, the opulence of the Norrington estate seemed to mock the sacrifices she was being asked to make.

Entering her bedroom, a sanctuary adorned with delicate lace and pastel hues, Lady Charlotte collapsed onto the plush chaise. The tears, silent yet poignant, flowed freely as she grappled with the reality of her situation. The dreams of marrying for love seemed to crumble around her, leaving behind a sense of desolation.

She gazed at her reflection in the ornate wooden mirror; her round face framed by the cascading curls of black hair. The once vibrant blue eyes now mirrored the turmoil within; a conflict between duty and desire, between the obligations to her family and the yearning for a man she loved.

Her ivory handkerchief, embroidered with delicate patterns, became a vessel for her silent lamentations. She mourned not only for the love she might never find but also for the loss of charting the course of her own destiny.

Chapter Two

The grand ballroom of the Duke and Duchess of Durham glittered with crystal chandeliers, casting a warm and ethereal glow over the assembled nobility dressed in finery. Charlotte, adorned in a resplendent gown of silvery-blue satin and delicate lace paired with satin slippers and elbow-length white gloves, moved through the swirling sea of dancers with forced grace. The whispers and glances that followed her reflected her lacklustre first season.

"Poor Lady Charlotte, destined to languish in the shadows once again," one lady sneered, her eyes assessing the perceived shortcomings of the reluctant debutante.

"True. One would think with her beauty and status, she would have hinged on a husband in her first season."

She didn't pay them any mind because they didn't know the reason she had rejected offers from suitors was because she didn't find a man that caught her fancy. Given what she had to do tonight, she wished she had picked any man.

"I hope she finds a husband before she gets left on the shelf."

Undeterred, Lady Charlotte maintained her composure, guided by etiquette ingrained in her from birth to withstand the biting remarks that accompanied her every step.

The Duke of Malvern, a man with greying temples and an imposing presence, was surrounded by men and women alike, all vying for his attention. Mothers stood with debutantes waiting to introduce to him.

Charlotte's mother, attired in an intricate ensemble of silk and lace, guided her towards the powerful duke. The air crackled with anticipation as Charlotte prepared to embark on the scripted dance of courtship.

The Duke, clad in a tailored coat of midnight black, snowy white shirt, with a silver cravat, and black trousers, finally turned to look at her.

"Your Grace, may I introduce my daughter, Lady Charlotte Norrington? She's the first daughter of the late Duke of Ravenswood."

Charlotte, her heart heavy with the weight of duty, curtsied with practiced elegance. She pasted a fake smile on her face as she stared at the older man with a square face, hooked nose, and grey beard. Masculine appreciation reflected in his brown eyes.

"May I have this dance, my lady?" he asked with an outstretched hand, shocking her and everyone around them. Her mother smiled brightly as Charlotte curtsied and the duke led her to the dance floor. Charlotte managed to hide her disappointment. She had secretly hoped that she wouldn't catch his fancy. Curse her beautiful features.

The dance began, a choreographed routine that mirrored the intricate social intricacies of Society. As the music swirled around them, Charlotte's gaze flitted across the crowded ballroom, searching for a flicker of genuine connection in the sea of people. The duke's conversation, steeped in societal pleasantries and obligatory flattery, failed to captivate her.

The scent of perfumed gloves and the rustle of silk gowns filled the air as the dance went on. An unspoken understanding passed between Charlotte and her mother when she caught her eye as the latter stood with her friends on the sidelines—a pact forged in whispers and familial obligation. It was time to execute the next phase of their plan.

Summoning the courage to endure the mundane exchanges, Charlotte initiated a polite inquiry. "Your Grace, the ballroom is delightful, but I find myself in need of a breath of fresh air. Would you be so kind as to accompany me to the garden?"

The duke agreed with a gracious smile. "As you wish, my lady."

Returning his smile, she placed her hand on his arm, and they waded through the crowded ballroom towards the open double doors. The moonlit garden, with its fragrant blossoms and secluded arbours, offered a brief respite from the stifling confines of the ballroom.

A gasp fell from Charlotte's lips when suddenly, she bumped into someone and felt moisture pooling on her dress.

"Oh! That's so clumsy of me. What a shame to have ruined such a lovely dress."

Charlotte glared at Lady Fitzgerald as she walked away, knowing very well that spilling punch on her dress wasn't a mistake. For reasons she couldn't understand, Emily had always hated her. Possibly because she was a duke's daughter while Emily was a lowly baron's daughter.

Gritting her teeth inwardly, Charlotte stopped herself from blistering her rival's ears with unladylike words.

Her rival's malicious act had not gone unnoticed, and the duke, with a furrowed brow, expressed his concern. "Lady Charlotte, it appears your dress has suffered an unfortunate mishap. Allow me to escort you back to the ballroom," he offered with a courteous tone.

Summoning her best facade of graciousness, Charlotte declined his offer, feigning a blush. "Your Grace, I appreciate your concern, but a lady must maintain her composure even in the face of such accidents. Please, wait for me in the arbour. I shall return shortly."

With that, she lifted the skirts of her dress and left the duke in the garden, his silhouette a stoic figure against the moonlit backdrop. Hurrying back to the ballroom and then to the retiring room, she sought assistance to remedy the punch-stained gown. Her mother sought her to ask what happened, and she told her about the petty vengeance of a jealous rival. Between them, they successfully wiped off the stain from the dress and Charlotte hastened back to the arbour, her heart pounding with a mix of apprehension and determination.

Under the watchful gaze of the stars, she approached the secluded spot. She felt the anticipation building within her as she aimed to navigate these uncharted waters with calculated precision. As she approached, she saw the outline of a figure in the moonlight, and her heart thundered against her chest for what she was about to do to the nice, old duke. Probably due to nervousness, she didn't see a small tree stump before her. She struck her satin slipper against it, and let out a small scream as she darted forward in a fall. The duke caught her immediately and held her tightly in his arms.

However, the arms that caught her were not those of the Duke of Malvern. The startled gasp that escaped Charlotte's lips was drowned by the presence of the man who held her—none other than the Duke of Banbury. The man she detested, the source of a history marred by disdain and resentment.

Caught in a compromising situation, Charlotte recoiled, her eyes meeting the stormy grey ones of the Duke of Banbury. The moonlight revealed a flicker of surprise and curiosity in his gaze.

In the shadows, her scheming accomplices, along with the famous gossips of the *ton*, emerged to witness the scene. The trap had been set, and the reluctant debutante found herself ensnared in a web of social intrigue, duty, and an unexpected encounter with the Duke of Banbury.

Chapter Three

The grandeur of the ballroom began to fade as Charlotte, escorted by her mother, made a hasty exit. The whispers and judgmental gazes of the *ton* followed them like a haunting melody, and the weight of the unfolding scandal settled heavily on Charlotte's shoulders.

The night air outside was cool, a stark contrast to the heated emotions swirling within her. The elegant ducal carriage awaited them, its polished exterior gleaming under the soft glow of streetlamps. Charlotte, still in shock, took a moment to glance around the deserted street, her mind reeling with the unexpected turn of events. Once inside the carriage, the reality of the situation bore down on Charlotte. Her mother sat beside her, her countenance etched with a mixture of disappointment and distress.

Had she really just seen the man who had made her heart flutter two years ago? With the moon bathing his face in its light, she had seen that he had become even more handsome than ever. Being in his arms had sent awakening shots up her body. But he was the worst person to be caught with.

As the carriage traversed the dimly lit streets, each turn taking them closer to their London townhouse on Emerald Street, Charlotte felt a sinking sensation in the pit of her stomach. The consequences of her actions were unravelling before her, like the intricate threads of a finely woven tapestry.

"How could you throw yourself into the arms of that...that rake?"

"Mother, I never intended for this to happen," Charlotte explained, her voice a delicate murmur in the confined space. "I mistook him for the Duke of Malvern. It was an honest mistake."

Her mother fixed her with a stern gaze. "Charlotte, do you realise the implications of what just occurred? The *ton* witnessed you in a compromising situation with the Duke of Banbury, a known libertine and rake."

"I assure you, Mother, I had no intention of—"

Her mother interrupted, her voice laced with a mixture of despair and frustration. "Intentions matter little in the eyes of Society, Charlotte. You've been seen with a man who, by reputation, mirrors the vices of your late father. A gambler, a blackguard, and a drunk!"

The mention of her father struck a chord within Charlotte. A man whose reckless behaviour had left the family in financial ruin and whose shadow still lingered over their lives. The Duke of Banbury's reputation, akin to her father's, cast a looming spectre over her future.

"But I didn't mean for it to happen. Curse that tree stump. If it weren't for it, I would have noticed he wasn't Duke Malvern and made a hasty retreat from his presence." She sighed. "I cannot marry a man with such a disreputable standing."

As the carriage rolled to a stop before the imposing two-storeyed building, the dowager duchess turned to her daughter with tear-filled eyes. "You must understand, Charlotte. Society will not forgive such a transgression. If you refuse the Duke of Banbury's advances, you will be ruined."

Charlotte, a mix of defiance and desperation in her gaze, retorted, "I would rather face ruin than be shackled to a man like him. I won't sacrifice my happiness for the sake of societal expectations."

Her mother's anguished expression deepened, the weight of their precarious situation settling heavily upon them. The wheels of destiny had been set in motion, and Charlotte's path was now entwined with a man whose reputation threatened to unravel the fragile threads of her future.

"We shall discuss it further in the drawing room."

The footman opened the carriage door and set down the step. Charlotte climbed out of the conveyance with the help of the older man. Lifting the skirts of her dress, she hurried into the house and the drawing room with her mother at her wake.

The flickering candlelight in the drawing room cast shadows on Charlotte's determined face as she contemplated the impending storm, pacing the carpeted floor. The clock on the mantelpiece ticked with ominous regularity, underscoring the gravity of the situation.

Her mother, her eyes moist from tears, looked at Charlotte with a mixture of maternal concern and resignation.

"Charlotte, my dearest," she began, "I implore you to reconsider. Our family's future hangs in the balance. Your sisters' prospects depend on the decisions we make now."

Charlotte's jaw clenched and her gaze hardened. She knew the weight of responsibility rested on her shoulders, but the memories of the Duke of Banbury's past actions fuelled her defiance. The man she detested, the man who had once made her a laughingstock amongst her peers, would not be the master of her fate.

"I cannot, Mother. You may not be aware of it, but I've met the Duke of Banbury before. Two years ago, at Lady Constance's birthday party," Charlotte revealed, her voice tinged with resentment. "He feigned interest in me and I accepted, only for him to be found kissing another woman moments later. In my anger, I made sure the *ton* knew of his indiscretions."

Her mother's eyes widened in shock. "Charlotte, why didn't you mention this before?"

"I thought our paths would never cross again. I was wrong," Charlotte confessed, her gaze fixed on the flickering flames. "Now, he holds the key to our family's salvation, or so it seems."

Charlotte sighed, realising the complexity of the predicament. The echoes of past grievances had resurfaced to intertwine with the family's desperate circumstances.

"Can you not find it within yourself to set aside personal grievances for the sake of your sisters?" she implored, her voice a gentle plea.

Charlotte's expression softened momentarily, revealing the internal struggle between duty and personal convictions. The prospect of sacrificing her happiness for the sake of her sisters weighed heavily on her, yet the bitter taste of resentment lingered.

"I will not be forced into such a union, Mother. I agreed to the plan of marrying Duke Malvern, but I cannot marry a man I despise, no matter the consequences," Charlotte declared, a spark of determination lighting her blue eyes. "I would rather drink poison than marry a man who humiliated me. I won't!"

And with that outburst, she hurried up the stairs to her room, where she flung herself on her bed. Why was life so unfair to her? It was bad enough that she had gone to the ball with the hope of ensnaring a man old enough to be her father, but now she was ensnared with a man she hated with a passion.

"It's so unfair," she sobbed.

Chapter Four

"Hurry, Lottie. He has been waiting for almost half an hour," Amelia, Charlotte's ten-and-seven immediate younger sister, urged as she tugged on her hand.

"Let him wait," Charlotte snapped as she refused to rise from the dresser stool.

Amelia beamed from ear to ear. "I think it's so romantic that you caught the interest of a duke on your first night in your second season. My, is he handsome!"

Fifteen-year-old Sophia, seated on the bed with a book in her hands as usual, rolled her eyes. "I prefer intellect to handsomeness."

Amelia waved a hand at her. "I think he's both."

Charlotte felt like letting out a scream that could wake up the dead. Half an hour ago, her mother and sisters had hurried into her room to awaken her because the Duke of Banbury had come calling. She had been shocked and then infuriated at his audacity. What did he want after trying to ruin her life? She had thought she would spend the whole day abed, mourning her future, but her mother and sisters would have none of that.

"Hurry, Lottie. We do not want him to lose interest because of your tardiness, do we? I mean, it's customary for a woman not to show too much eagerness, but being excessively tardy isn't fashionable either."

To avoid hearing the prattle of her younger sister any further, Charlotte pushed herself to her feet and exited the room with Amelia on her heels.

The morning sun cast a golden glow over the townhouse as Charlotte descended the grand staircase, her steps unhurried.

Dressed in a gown of muted lavender silk, she presented a picture of subdued elegance. The gown, adorned with delicate lace and ribbon, was a testament to her societal standing. Her sisters, Amelia and Sophia, flanked her, their presence both supportive and apprehensive.

The drawing room, with its high ceilings and opulent furnishings, served as the backdrop for this unexpected meeting. Antique furniture, draped in rich fabrics, bore witness to the centuries-old history of the Norrington family.

As she entered the room, she found the Duke of Banbury standing by the French windows, his tall frame outlined against the streaming sunlight. Anthony Witherspoon, impeccably attired in a tailored dark coat, light blue shirt, dark blue cravat, and black trousers and boots, turned to face her, twirling a black hat in his hand. His penetrating grey eyes held a mixture of determination and perhaps a hint of something deeper. Midnight black hair, angular face, stormy grey eyes, a Grecian nose, and a neatly trimmed beard were a testament to his aristocratic origin.

Charlotte forced herself to dip a curtsy just as her sisters did before they left the room. She almost called them back for support, but she didn't want them to know the embarrassment she suffered at the hands of this man years ago, which would most likely come up.

"Your Grace, to what do I owe the...pleasure of your visit?" she inquired, her voice laced with a restrained formality.

Anthony regarded her with a steady gaze. "Lady Charlotte, we find ourselves in a most unfortunate circumstance. I have refrained from demanding satisfaction in a duel with your brother, for I do not wish to stain my hands with the blood of kin. However, the matter at hand is non-negotiable."

Her brows furrowed in confusion. "What matter, Your Grace?"

He paced slightly as if contemplating how to articulate the delicate situation. "Do not feign ignorance, my lady. It doesn't suit you."

Charlotte shrugged with stubbornness. "I do not know what you speak of, Your Grace."

With a grim smile, he said, "Very well then. We'll play your game of denial. However, the unfortunate situation we found ourselves in last night has to be remedied by you becoming my wife."

Charlotte's eyes widened, a mixture of disbelief and defiance flashing in their blue depths. "Marry you? Over my dead body!"

Anthony sighed, his expression firm. "I have chosen not to escalate this matter with your family for the sake of avoiding scandal. Refusing to comply may result in consequences neither of us desires."

Too incensed for words, she made to disrespect him by walking away, but he caught up with her before she reached the door and held her arm. Something foreign and inexplicable shot through Charlotte as she raised her head to look at him. The tension in the room escalated, and the chemistry between them crackled with unspoken challenges.

Charlotte's cheeks flushed with a mixture of anger and frustration. However, she stood her ground, defiance etched into every line of her countenance. The room, once a sanctuary of familial warmth, now hosted a clash of wills between two formidable figures.

Anthony's gaze bore into hers, his eyes reflecting the steely resolve that had earned him a formidable reputation in the *ton*. She had always known that the Duke of Banbury, known for his unwavering determination, was not a man easily swayed.

"Unhand me, Your Grace," she finally said when she could no longer withstand the intensity of his heated gaze.

"Then behave yourself as befitting the stature of a lady...and a future duchess," he replied with a smirk before releasing her.

Charlotte snorted in an unladylike fashion. "Your Grace, I will not be coerced into an unwanted marriage," she retorted, her voice carrying the weight of her unwavering spirit.

Anthony's lips curled into a cold smile. "Unwanted, Lady Charlotte? This is a matter of honour and redemption. I refuse to be tarnished further by baseless accusations, and you will rectify the damage you inflicted on my name two years ago."

She flushed and looked away. "I do not know what you speak of."

He raised a brow. "You don't? You don't remember starting the rumour of me being a despoiler of innocents and a rogue?" He folded his arms across his chest. "Pray tell, why did you do it?"

With her face turning a deeper shade of red, Charlotte turned away. How could she tell him that it was because he had spurned her for another woman that pushed her into telling anyone who cared to listen lies about him?

"I insist that I do not know what you're talking about. Any reputation you have was duly earned by you."

"Oh, really?"

As the verbal spar continued, the room felt smaller, the atmosphere charged with the clash of conflicting emotions. Charlotte, though defiant, could not ignore the weight of her family's precarious situation. Anthony, certainly aware of his advantage, pressed on with an intensity that mirrored the flames of their verbal exchange.

"You may despise me for a reason known to you, Lady Charlotte, but circumstances demand that we put aside personal grievances for the greater good. A scandal would be detrimental to both our families. I suggest you consider the consequences of refusing."

Charlotte gritted her teeth. A refusal to comply with Anthony's proposal would undoubtedly lead to her ruin, a fact not lost on either party.

She raised her eyes to look at him and her lips parted at the intensity of his stormy grey gaze. It was hardly a wonder why she had found him irresistibly handsome and accepted his proposal to court her years ago. The chemistry between them, once ignited by a twist of fate, now simmered beneath the surface, a potent mixture of animosity and unspoken tension.

"I will marry you, come what may." He positioned his hat on his head and gave her a cold smile. "Good day, my lady."

With a final stern look, he turned on his heel, leaving her to grapple with the reality of her predicament.

Chapter Five

As Charlotte descended the elegant staircase adorned with a plush burgundy carpet, her eyes caught the intricate details of the crystal chandelier that hung above the foyer.

She walked into the breakfast room, where William and their mother awaited her. The air was laced with a faint fragrance of fresh flowers. Charlotte took her seat at the polished mahogany table, her thoughts a tumultuous whirlwind. The clinking of silverware against fine china was accompanied by a heavy silence, broken only by the occasional rustle of papers as William perused the morning news.

Charlotte stared at the plate of toast and eggs in front of her and she sighed heavily. The thought of food was the furthest in her mind, given her predicament. She had hardly slept a wink the previous night thinking about her options. She wished she could run away, but what would happen to Amelia and Sophia? Amelia looked forward to her coming out season the following year, but with no dowry, her sister might not get the happily ever after that she craved.

But can I marry Anthony just to save my family? I detest him.

As if sensing her discomfiture, her mother turned to her, reached out, and squeezed her hand on the white lace tablecloth.

"Charlotte, we understand the sacrifice we ask of you," she began, her eyes betraying the gravity of the situation. "It's not just the family name at stake, but yours and your sisters' futures as well."

Charlotte nodded solemnly, her gaze fixed on the delicate porcelain cup of tea cradled in her hands. The weight of responsibility pressed down on her shoulders, an unspoken burden that threatened to crush the dreams of a love once cherished.

William cleared his throat before addressing her. "The Duke of Banbury has requested a carriage ride with you. It would be in our best interest to foster a connection."

Charlotte's eyes darkened with a mixture of resentment and resignation. She had expected as much but couldn't shake the bitterness that clung to her.

With a deep sigh that reflected her inner feelings, she nodded. She didn't have a choice, did she? If she didn't marry Anthony, she would be ruined. The scandal would cause a stain on the Norrington name and her sisters would find it difficult to find a perfect match, especially with little or no dowry. Whether she married him or not, Charlotte would never have the chance of finding the love she so desperately craved.

"I will marry the duke," she finally said.

Her mother and brother beamed with delight. Her mother reached out to hug her while William smiled at her.

"Thank you, Charlotte, for doing this for your family. One can only hope that Duke Banbury will fare better than your father and not leave you in this same predicament that I find myself at his demise."

William nodded. "Thank you, Charlotte. Your sacrifice is greatly appreciated."

Later, Charlotte prepared to face the man she had once thought she loved, with Amelia fussing over her. Attired in a powder blue satin dress, she descended the stairs to the foyer where Anthony awaited her with a composed countenance. The intricate embroidery of his coat and the subtle gleam of polished boots bespoke a man accustomed to the luxuries of aristocratic life.

"Your Grace," Charlotte greeted with a curtsy, her gaze meeting his with a guarded intensity.

"Lady Charlotte," Anthony replied, a glint of something she couldn't decipher in his eyes. "You look ravishing in that dress. I thought a leisurely carriage ride would afford us the opportunity to become better acquainted."

She gave him a cool smile before placing a hand on his arm as he led her out of the house. She caught a whiff of his cedar scent. He handed her into the open carriage before sitting beside her.

The wheels of the carriage began to turn, propelling them into a journey fraught with unspoken challenges. As the elegant vehicle rolled through the manicured landscape, Charlotte wondered what they could possibly say to each other. Silently, they traversed the scenic route to the park. She ignored the curious glances they got from passers-by. No doubt it would be all over London before the day was over that they had been seen together again.

The park grounds provided the backdrop for the carriage ride, with lush greenery and vibrant blooms that framed the path ahead and gigantic trees offering shades for the visitors. The rhythmic clip-clop of horse hooves echoed through the air. The subtle play of sunlight through the trees cast a warm glow on Lady Charlotte's countenance, emphasising the blue of her eyes that betrayed both defiance and a burgeoning fascination at the expert way he handled the horses.

Anthony, with his characteristic cool demeanour, attempted to engage her in light conversation. "Thankfully, the park isn't crowded. I had feared that we would be swamped with people," he remarked, his eyes glancing over the sprawling landscape.

Charlotte, initially guarded, found herself relenting to the allure of the tranquil scenery. The velvety green of the lawns and the vibrant hues of blooming flowers created a serene backdrop for their shared journey.

"'Tis fortunate, Your Grace."

He turned to her when she didn't say anything further. "Given that we're courting and will most definitely end up as husband and wife, I suggest you withhold formalities and call me by my given name."

Surprised, she turned to look at him. A gentle breeze tousled her ebony locks as she contemplated her companion. Anthony's gaze, inscrutable yet laced with a hint of genuine interest, met hers. She sensed the undercurrent of scrutiny, an unspoken acknowledgment of the intricacies that bound them.

"Very well then...Anthony."

He beamed at her. "That wasn't so bad, was it? And you don't have to look as if you're at a funeral, Charlotte. As we've found ourselves in such a precarious situation, I suggest we make the best of it."

Reluctantly, she nodded. "If you say so," she said taking his hand to disembark from the carriage.

As they strolled through the park, Anthony extended an arm, offering an illusion of camaraderie that belied the reality of their situation. Charlotte, her heart at war with her principles, hesitated before tentatively accepting his gesture.

The hushed whispers of Society, like delicate petals carried by the wind, reached their ears. Anthony's reputation as a charming rogue and Charlotte's once-scandalous encounter intertwined, creating an unexpected spectacle for the watchful eyes of their voyeurs.

"Ignore them," Anthony advised as they passed by two ladies standing beside a tree and whispering behind their palms.

"It's hard to do so, given that we're the centre of attention."

He nodded. "I would have said it was a mistake coming here, but we need to be seen in Society to show them we have nothing to be ashamed of. We did no wrong, and if you would stop looking like a victim and appear as if you're totally enjoying yourself in my presence, I believe we can pull it off and shame them for judging us."

Stunned, she glanced at him to see his watchful eyes on her. "I am not in a jovial mood to pretend so."

He gave her a stiff smile. "Why? Because I'm a libertine? A ne'er-do-well?"

"No. I don't mean that. I—"

He grinned. "I was merely jesting, my lady. Do not take life so seriously."

She lowered her head. "Tis easy for you to say. You're fortunate to have your gender at birth to do whatever you wish. It is not so for the supposed fairer sex."

He gazed at her with surprise. "Do you mean to tell me you reject being born a female?"

"But of course. What can a lady boast of except having a husband and a horde of children?"

Laughter bubbled from his throat. "Do you mean to tell me that males fare better than females? Males who carry the burden of their families and have to provide for them, come what may?"

She snorted. "But of course."

A hearty argument ensued between them. For a man who was rumoured to be a libertine, Charlotte discovered that he had an intelligent mind and made a compelling argument. They argued back and forth, completely forgetting about the people around them who kept whispering as they passed by.

By the time Anthony bade her goodbye an hour later, Charlotte was surprised to discover that she had actually enjoyed his company. Mayhap being married to him might not be so dreadful, after all.

Chapter Six

Tears glistened in Charlotte's eyes as she regretted coming to the Remington ball. She should never have listened to her mother, who talked her into coming to the ball and not hiding away as if she had something to be ashamed of. Ever since she and her mother were announced by the Remington butler with a booming voice, she had been treated as if she had the plague. No one spoke to her or asked her to dance. Instead, she was treated to hushed murmurs and sidelong glances.

"Mother, I think we should leave," Charlotte whispered to the dowager duchess who was standing with her friends.

Her mother turned to fix compassionate eyes on her. "No, Charlotte. Best we withstand their criticism than cower in shame."

We? What is she talking about? I'm the one being ostracised.

Charlotte saw Emily dancing with the Duke of Malvern. Only decorum ingrained in her from birth stopped her from going to get a glass of punch and spilling it on Emily's peach dress. She had learnt that Emily had waylaid the duke before he got to the arbour and led him back into the ballroom for a dance. Emily was the reason she was in this present predicament.

Suddenly, Charlotte's breath caught in her throat when the Duke of Banbury was announced by the butler. Her gaze immediately shot to the winding staircase where the tall, broad-shouldered man attired in all-black clothing which accentuated the strength of his body, was descending.

His entrance into the ballroom elicited a subtle shift in the atmosphere. Conversations faltered, and curious gazes followed his every step. It was hardly surprising that people thrust forward to talk to him. However, he ignored all of them and made a beeline for Charlotte. Her heart thundered against her chest as he drew abreast. His eyes, a piercing shade of grey, met hers with a silent reassurance that transcended the constraints of societal expectations. The searing gaze made her feel as if she was the only lady in the vast ballroom.

As Anthony approached Charlotte, a subtle tension enveloped them, a silent acknowledgment of the unspoken connection forged during their walk in the park.

Finally, he reached her and gave her his usual cold smile after a heated masculine appraisal of her figure.

"Charlotte, you're easily the most beautiful lady in this room tonight. I feel honoured to declare that I know you."

Charlotte couldn't help blushing as she curtsied. "Your... I mean, Anthony."

It was noted by the peer of the realms that both of them seemed to be on quite friendly terms and the duke didn't bother with propriety by greeting the people who stood around her. Instead, he only had eyes for her.

"Allow me the pleasure of this dance, Charlotte," Anthony said, extending a gloved hand with an elegance that belied the whispers surrounding his reputation.

Her gloved hand readily met his in a seamless fusion, and he led her to the dance floor through the throng of people staring at them and whispering.

The dance commenced, a waltz that echoed the intricate steps of their evolving connection. The gilded walls of the ballroom bore witness to their perfection as their spectators watched on.

The chemistry between them, an amalgamation of tension and an unspoken understanding, was palpable. The *ton*, momentarily silenced by the unconventional pairing, watched Charlotte navigate the dance floor with the enigmatic Duke of Banbury.

"Why are you doing this?" Charlotte couldn't suppress the question that lingered in the air between them.

"Doing what?" he asked, swirling her in his arms to the rhythm of the waltz.

"You barely acknowledged anyone, but came straight to ask me to dance. Surely you must know that we are now the topic of discussion."

He raised a brow. "Just like you were before I arrived?"

She frowned. "How did you know?"

"I stood on the landing for a long while, watching how the fickle people treated you."

Her face paled. "Oh. So it's out of pity, then?"

Anthony, his lips curved in an enigmatic smile. "Pity? I don't think I know the meaning of the word. Maybe philandering, gambling, or possibly cavorting with denigrates."

She couldn't help the giggle that burst from her lips.

"Now, that's better. Never allow such fickle people to dictate your feelings."

"Is that what you do?"

He nodded. "Yes, coupled with the fact that I am indeed every unprintable name they call me."

Laughter shook her shoulders.

"You have a musical laugh that calms the soul, gladdens the heart, and puts a smile on one's face."

The chandelier's crystalline radiance reflected in his grey eyes, leaving Charlotte momentarily entranced. In that fleeting moment, the weight of societal expectations seemed to dissipate, leaving only the undeniable chemistry that simmered beneath the surface.

She lowered her gaze; her face flushed. "One would never have thought that you could be so poetic. But then again, as a rake, your words would be strewn with honey."

He threw back his head and laughter bubbled from his throat, causing warmth to spread all over her. Their onlookers gazed at them with awe, sensing how much they seemed to be enjoying each other's company.

He shook his head after containing his hilarity. "I merely spoke the truth. You should laugh more often. It suits you."

Her eyes twinkled with mischief. "Why, thank you, Your Grace."

The waltz concluded with a final, graceful twirl, leaving Charlotte breathless yet strangely exhilarated. As the *ton* parted a way for them, he guided her away from the dance floor.

"Tell me why you have been so nice to me," Charlotte pressed as they walked away from the prying eyes of the crowd.

"Why indeed?" Anthony finally responded, his voice a low murmur meant for her ears alone. The ballroom buzzed with conversations, yet their private exchange remained shielded from the curious gazes.

Charlotte, torn between distrust and a burgeoning attraction, found herself searching for answers within the depths of his gaze. His silence, both maddening and intriguing, only fuelled the burgeoning mystery that surrounded the Duke of Banbury.

As the music continued to weave its enchantment, Charlotte realised that, despite her reservations, the dance had unravelled something within her – a complex tapestry of emotions that blurred the lines between duty and desire. The *ton* might judge, but at that moment, she knew something had changed between them. That he had come to her rescue warmed her heart because, after he handed her to her mother, the eyes of the crowd didn't seem so judgmental again. When he came to ask for a second dance and she obliged against propriety, whispers began to filter into her ears that they might indeed be secretly betrothed as they had heard.

"Was that your doing? Making them think we're already betrothed, hence why we were caught in the arbour?"

He shrugged as he twirled her around the dance floor. "If they are capricious enough to be swayed by speaking certain words into the ears of men who don't know how to keep things to themselves, mayhap they deserve to be deceived."

A soft giggle of laughter burst from her throat. "You're incorrigible."

He shook his head. "No. I'm determined."

She wondered at the weightiness of his tone. Something told her that he was toying with her, playing a game that might hurt her again.

However, she couldn't deny the pull she felt for him, and with his charm, she saw why she instantly fell for him two years ago.

That night, as she lay on her bed exhausted, she went through the events of the night and how Anthony made her heart flutter. One thing she was certain of was that her feelings towards him were beginning to change, but she had to be careful because she didn't think she could trust him.

Chapter Seven

Over the next few weeks, Charlotte and Anthony attended several soirees together. Whenever they were seen at any Venetian breakfast, birthday party, musicale, tongues wagged uncontrollably. Charlotte found herself enjoying both Anthony's company and the attention that their presence together drew.

The malleable nobles had forgiven her indiscretion of cavorting with a man alone and in the dark because they thought that she and Anthony were madly in love with each other...or so they thought. Charlotte couldn't deny that she had started developing feelings for Anthony against her wishes. He was charming, attentive, and considerate, and made her feel as if she was the most desirable lady in all of England; everything she wanted in a man. But she still didn't trust him. She suspected there was a reason he was paying so much attention to her. However, she had surmised that he wasn't quite the libertine that people had portrayed him to be. He was intelligent, hardworking, and well-read. She decided to find out the truth the night they attended Lady Bloomfield's ball.

The ballroom buzzed with vibrant conversations as Charlotte, accompanied by the enigmatic Anthony, made a grand entrance into the glittering world of London's high Society. The *ton*, ever eager for scandal and romance, watched with rapt attention as the pair, once embroiled in a scandal of their own, navigated the dance floor with effortless grace.

The attire of the elite shimmered in the ambient glow of crystal chandeliers, the ladies adorned in gowns of silk and satin that whispered with each delicate step. Charlotte's gown, a vision in midnight blue, accentuated her slender frame, the intricate lace trailing along the hem adding an air of regal sophistication. Beside her, Anthony cut a striking figure in a well-tailored burgundy coat, snowy white frilled shirt, and black trousers.

As they swirled through the intricate patterns of a quadrille, the onlookers speculated about the nature of their relationship. Gossip flowed like champagne, painting a narrative of the growing love affair between them.

Amidst the swirling sea of dancers, Charlotte couldn't escape the watchful eyes of Society, both intrigued and sceptical. The subtle nods and knowing smiles from acquaintances hinted at a tacit approval, a shift in perception that acknowledged her redemption through the unexpected alliance with the duke.

As the evening unfolded, Anthony led Charlotte through the various dance forms, each movement a testament to the chemistry that continued to blossom between them. The peers of the realm, eager for a love story, created their narratives and lapped up the beautiful match that they made.

In a brief respite between dances, Anthony escorted Charlotte to a secluded alcove graced with cascading ivy. The soft glow of candlelight accentuated the intimacy of their conversation, shielded from the prying eyes of the ballroom.

"Your dance card is nearly full for the evening, my lady," Anthony remarked, his tone a low murmur that resonated with a hint of amusement. "It appears that our peers are quite enamoured with our newfound...alliance."

Charlotte, her cheeks rosy with a delicate flush, met Anthony's gaze with a mixture of uncertainty and increasing affection. "It's all a charade, isn't it? A dance of appearances to salvage my reputation."

Anthony nodded thoughtfully. "Indeed, the *ton* revels in its love for a good spectacle. But, Charlotte, I cannot deny that there might be truth buried within the charade."

"Truth? The truth is that your reputation precedes you, Duke of Banbury," she replied, her words layered with a cautious acknowledgment. "The gossip mill has been whispering tales of your exploits and rakish charm. Why, then, would you choose to court a lady burdened by scandal?"

"Is it so difficult to believe that a man might seek a genuine connection, Charlotte?" Anthony's voice, a velvet murmur, held a trace of humor. "In this intricate dance of courtship, motives may be multifaceted, but the heart, when laid bare, seeks authenticity."

She snorted at his reply. "I asked a simple question, Anthony. Why are you courting a supposed scandalous lady?"

Anthony's gaze held a flicker of amusement as if relishing the challenge of unscrambling the enigma that Charlotte presented. "Scandal is a fickle companion, my lady. It weaves its narrative based on half-truths and fleeting moments. Perhaps, in this elaborate dance, I seek to rewrite the script, to unveil the woman behind the whispers."

She looked at him with disbelief and he sighed.

"Charlotte, I understand the scepticism that shrouds my intentions," Anthony began, his words chosen with meticulous care. "But if you permit me, allow this courtship to be a testament to the possibility of redemption, for both of us."

She studied him, the flickering candlelight casting shadows on his features. "Redemption, Anthony? What sins do you seek to absolve, and why involve me in this endeavour?"

Anthony gave her the usual cold smile that she hated. "The sins of my past are layered, and in you, I see the potential for a shared journey of forgiveness and renewal. Your scandal need not define you, Charlotte, just as my reputation need not dictate my future."

"So, you're courting me to clear your name and mine?"

"That would seem to be the case."

"Then why don't I believe you?"

He shrugged. "Mayhap you have allowed the tales of gossips to form an erroneous judgment of me."

Given the weeks they had spent together and how she discovered he was nothing at all what she had heard of him, even though she had been a part of the rumourmongers, she nodded.

As Anthony led her back to the ball, Charlotte grudgingly decided that she would trust him. After all, she was beginning to see him in a new light.

"One more thing," he said as he steered her through the throng of people to her mother. "I'm courting you because I need a bride."

Charlotte's breath caught sharply in her throat.

He nodded. "Amidst the grandeur and the gaiety of the Remington ball, I realized the importance of finding a bride who values more than just the title and the wealth. But enough of this talk, let us return to your mama before she wonders at our absence."

Chapter Eight

"If I didn't know any better, I would say you are in love, my dear," the Dowager Duchess of Ravenswood teased as she enjoyed afternoon tea with her daughters in the drawing room.

Charlotte blushed. "Mother!"

Amelia beamed. "Their courtship is on everyone's lips. It's a known fact how much the two of you love each other."

Charlotte rolled her eyes at Amelia's fondness for the news of a love match between two people. Sophia sat quietly near the fireplace, reading a book as usual.

"My only fear is that he might be like your father," her mother mentioned quietly.

Charlotte snorted. "Mother, Anthony is not like Father at all. He's a gentleman, hardworking, and very intelligent. I believe he's sincere in his intentions," Charlotte asserted, her eyes reflecting a confidence that had replaced her initial scepticism.

Her mother studied her with a mixture of maternal concern and teasing amusement. "And you say you're not in love with him when you rise so expertly to his defence? My dear Charlotte, love has a way of transforming uncertainty into unwavering faith. You defend him as if your heart has already made its choice."

Charlotte blushed, her cheeks tinged with the rosy hues of affection.

There was no need to deny it any further. "Perhaps, Mother, my heart has indeed made its choice. Anthony has proven himself honourable, and I find solace in his company."

Amelia clapped her hands with glee. "Oh. That's so beautiful, Lottie."

Her mother stared at her keenly. "So, duty isn't so distasteful anymore, is it?"

Still blushing, Charlotte shook her head. "No, it isn't."

She was no longer averse to marrying him. As a matter of fact, she yearned for him to ask the question. Perhaps, at the dinner party for the Earl of Shelton's birthday, he might ask her what her heart most desired.

Hours later, Charlotte, draped in a gown of pale yellow silk, moved with grace and poise, a vision of regal beauty. The elaborate lace embellishments cascaded down the gown, catching the light in a mesmerising dance. Her midnight curls were elegantly arranged, adorned with a delicate yellow tiara that sparkled like stars.

Anthony made a striking figure in a tailored black coat adorned with silver embroidery. The flickering candlelight accentuated the chiselled lines of his angular face, and the faint hint of a smile played on his lips as he escorted Charlotte out of the dining hall. They had just partaken of a sumptuous feast in honour of the earl. Now, guests glided to the ballroom to dance to the entertaining music from musicians in a corner of the opulent space.

Their chemistry, once a silent undercurrent, now bubbled to the surface, a subtle exchange of glances, a shared laughter that echoed through the ballroom. As they moved in harmony with the music, Charlotte felt a warmth blossom within her. Anthony's presence, once a source of apprehension, now offered solace and familiarity.

As the evening unfolded, Anthony and Charlotte shared a waltz that transcended the dance floor. The sweeping melodies of the orchestra intertwined with their laughter and conversations, creating an enchanting atmosphere.

"I never thought I would find such joy in a dance," Anthony admitted, his gaze fixed on Charlotte.

She smiled, the dimples on her cheeks adding to the allure of her countenance. "Nor did I, Anthony."

"Perhaps we should repair to the garden for some fresh air. You look flushed," he suggested.

She nodded. "I must first visit the retiring room, though."

"Very well. I shall wait for your return by the door to escort you."

Beaming, Charlotte lifted her skirts and hurried away from the ballroom. Everything in her told her he wanted to ask her to marry him. So, she quickly visited the powder room and moved hastily back to the ballroom, ignoring anyone who wanted to stop her for a conversation about her courtship with Anthony.

She frowned when she didn't see him by the double doors. Perhaps he had gone ahead of her to secure a place on one of the benches. Smiling, she walked out of the ballroom.

The moonlit garden, bathed in silver hues, provided a serene retreat from the lively ballroom. Charlotte, with her gown trailing lightly behind her, sought solace amidst the fragrant blossoms and winding pathways. The delicate scent of roses lingered in the air. She heard voices in the arbour and walked in its direction.

"I say, Banbury. Your plan to woo Lady Charlotte has worked splendidly," someone said, which caused Charlotte's steps to falter.

"What plan?" she heard another voice ask.

"Banbury is only after her huge dowry."

She clamped a hand across her mouth to suppress a gasp.

"He has been pretending to her just so she would accept his proposal and marry him. After their wedding, he would dump her in one of his properties and carry on with his philandering ways. Well, I must say his plan has worked superbly, and not only would he be getting a huge dowry, but she would also be paying for spreading false rumours about him."

The revelation hit Charlotte like a sudden tempest, shattering the illusion of happiness that had enveloped her these past weeks. Having heard enough, she turned away.

He's only after my dowry... pretending to be someone he's not. He's really a libertine! A scoundrel of the worst kind!

Heart pounding as she walked away, she struggled to reconcile the man she believed Anthony to be with the one revealed in that fateful conversation. The moon, witness to her silent suffering, cast its silvery glow upon her tear-streaked face.

Hurt and betrayal waged war within her, and she realised that the delicate threads of trust she had woven around Anthony were untying. Running through the moonlit garden, the world blurred as tears mingled with the petals strewn along her path. Her sobs, a mournful melody, echoed through the night as she sought refuge deeper in the garden from the painful revelation.

Chapter Nine

"Charlotte, dearest sister, you cannot allow this heartbreak to define you," Amelia implored, her voice a comforting lullaby amid despair.

Charlotte raised her tear-stained face from her wet pillow. "What will you have me do, Amelia?" She sniffed and dabbed at her eyes with her delicate handkerchief. "Anthony has wrenched my heart from my chest and thrown it away like nothing."

Amelia nodded in agreement, her blue eyes reflecting the unwavering support she offered. "I understand, but you deserve more than the betrayal he has shown. Do not let the actions of one man cast a shadow over the love you are truly worthy of."

Charlotte's shoulders shook and more sobs wracked her slim frame. She wished she hadn't gone into the garden the previous night to listen to that heartbreaking revelation, but then again, it was best that she knew now than to marry him and live like a prisoner in his home. But the pain of his betrayal seemed too much for her to bear, especially as she had fallen hopelessly in love with him.

Just then, Sophia came into the room to announce that Anthony had come to call on her.

"The gall of him! What more does he want? To drive the knife further in my chest?"

"Mayhap if you confront him and tell him to his face that you know his plans, it would shame him," Sophia suggested.

"Of what use would it be?" Charlotte dabbed at her eyes. "Tell him to go away and never come back. I'd rather marry a man old enough to even be my grandfather than marry a lying scoundrel!"

"Oh, Lottie!" Amelia threw her arms around her as tears poured down from her own face. "Please stop crying. All will be well."

Charlotte remained resolute in her anguish for days. No one could comfort her. The ache in her chest seemed to consume her whole. William desired to go and call Anthony out for a duel for doing this to her, but she begged him not to, for it would cause another scandal. He apologised profusely, for if he hadn't brought up the plan to put her in a compromising position with Duke Malvern, she wouldn't have fallen into his scheming arms.

She hated that she missed attending soirees with him, conversing with him on various topics, and dancing with him. But she would rather remain on the shelf than marry such a despicable man.

The hushed tones of the *ton*, ever-eager to devour the latest scandal, buzzed with speculation about Charlotte's sudden withdrawal from society. Anthony repeatedly called on her but she refused to see him. She feared that because she loved him so much, he would come to her with flowery words and she would believe him.

Charlotte wished she could lock herself away in her room forever but she remembered that duty called. Her family still needed her to marry a wealthy husband, so she wouldn't fail them even though her heart had been shattered to a thousand pieces in her quest to fulfil her duty to her family.

Although she despised doing it, Charlotte, attired in a peach silk gown with puffed slips and a low neckline with lace trimmings, flirted with every gentleman that paid her attention at the Hartington ball that night. With a heavy heart, she approached the Duke of Malvern when Emily finally got her claws off him to dance with another man. Hardly had she reached him when the butler announced the Duke of Banbury. Her gaze darted to the top of the stairs, where Anthony descended with a determined look on his face. Just like after the scandal broke, he ignored everyone else as soon as he entered the vast ballroom and walked straight up to her. To her chagrin, the older duke smiled and walked away. Gossips had already been speculating that they had a lover's tiff, so it was hardly surprising that she and Anthony became the cynosure for all eyes when he reached her.

Her eyes met Anthony's piercing gaze, and her heart wrenched with despair again. Why did he have to be so cruel? How could she love a man so despicable? A tension, palpable and charged, hung in the air, suffocating the once-genteel ambiance of the ball. In the dimly lit corners of the room, whispers of their tumultuous connection reverberated like haunting echoes.

"Good evening, Charlotte," Anthony greeted with a cool smile.

Charlotte donned an impermeable mask of indifference. "Good evening, Your Grace. Mind you, you no longer have leave to use my first name, given that we are no longer…acquainted," she replied, her voice laced with a feigned sweetness that masked the turmoil within.

His lips thinned. "I have been trying to see you for over a week now. What's amiss? Why did you leave Shelton's party so abruptly? Were you ill?" His grey eyes held concern, which she found annoying. "Have you been ill? Is that why you have refused to see me? Or have I done something wrong?" Glancing around him at the unabashed interest of the people standing around them, he lowered his voice. "I believe we need to discuss this in private. We—"

Before he could finish, Charlotte, with a cold smile playing on her lips, interrupted him. "Your Grace, there is nothing left to discuss between us. It appears my previous judgment of your character was grievously mistaken."

Anthony, his brows furrowed in confusion, implored, "What are you talking about?"

"Do not pretend not to know what I speak of, Your Grace. I am fully aware of the reasons why you have been courting me. Your friends had a jolly time laughing at my expense."

Comprehension dawned and he frowned thickly. "Charlotte, please allow me to explain."

In response, she unleashed a torrent of words, each one a sharp arrow aimed at the heart of his pride. "Explanations are unnecessary, Your Grace. You were a means to an end – a pawn in my game to salvage my family's fortunes. It's rather amusing, really, how easily one can manipulate a man blinded by his own arrogance."

The ballroom, once alive with the strains of a waltz, now echoed with the resounding thud of Charlotte's cutting words. The onlookers, previously ensnared by the allure of the dance, became unwitting spectators to a spectacle of shattered illusions.

Anthony, his countenance a mask of wounded pride, recoiled at her audacious revelation.

"I do not require your false attention on me, anymore. It turns out that there are better men I should have approached than you. My mistake."

With a curt nod, Charlotte turned away, leaving Anthony in the wake of her verbal assault. The air, thick with tension, crackled with the remnants of their shattered connection. As Charlotte retreated into the shadowed alcoves of the ballroom, the resolute set of her jaw betrayed the turmoil within – a storm of conflicting emotions raging beneath the veneer of composure. It took everything in her not to hide somewhere and cry her eyes out. Her heart clenched with longing and despondency when she observed from the corner of her eye as Anthony left the ballroom. She ached to call him back and accept whatever explanation he gave to her, but she would be foolish to do that. It was for the best that she found another suitor. This time around, she would keep her heart out of it.

Chapter Ten

A few days later, Charlotte, clad in a gown of soft lavender, ambled through the manicured pathways alongside her sisters. Their laughter, a harmonious melody, mingled with the rustle of leaves and the distant trill of songbirds. She wondered why she had allowed them to talk her into taking a walk as she kept catching the inquisitive eyes of passers-by. Her altercation with Anthony hadn't gone unnoticed, and she wished she had been more diplomatic in handling it. Although she had gained satisfaction from giving him the cut, her heart still ached from loving him.

Amelia twirled her parasol behind her. "Do not worry, Lottie, a better man will mend your broken heart."

Sophia snickered. "Why do you always carry on so with love and happily ever after?"

Amelia giggled. "And why can't you get your nose out of a book?"

"Touché," Sophia replied and laughed.

Charlotte wished she could be as jovial as her sisters. Unexpectedly, a carriage pulled up with stately grace beside them. Her eyes widened when she saw the shiny gold ducal emblem of The Duke of Banbury on the black door. Her sisters exchanged curious glances, their steps slowing as anticipation swirled in the air.

Anthony, resplendent in a dark blue tailored coat that accentuated the aristocratic lines of his frame, alighted from the carriage. His gaze, an intense fusion of remorse and sincerity, locked onto Charlotte. Her heart missed a beat at the force of his gaze.

"Charlotte," Anthony began, his voice a low, earnest cadence that carried through the air. "May I have a moment of your time?"

Charlotte, guarded yet intrigued, inclined her head in acquiescence. Her sisters looked at each other with excitement before moving backward to give them some privacy.

Anthony stepped closer, his eyes searching hers for a glimmer of understanding. "I owe you an apology, one that words alone can scarcely convey. I jest not when I declare that I love you, Charlotte, and have loved you since the moment our paths first crossed two years ago."

What? Were her ears failing her? Was that an avowal of love from him?

Charlotte, though outwardly composed, betrayed a flicker of vulnerability.

Anthony continued, his words fervent. "The jovial banter with my friends, the jests about my mother's relentless pursuit of a bride; they were but a façade, a mask I wore to conceal the truth. I am earnest in my affections, Charlotte, and I can no longer bear the charade."

All she could do was gawk at him.

"My friends told me I would fall hopelessly in love with you again like I did two years ago, but to save face, I told them those lies because they knew how much it broke me when you spread lies about me. I would never do that to you, Charlotte."

Charlotte, her eyes fixed upon Anthony's, absorbed the gravity of his words. She desperately wanted to believe him, but she feared getting hurt again.

"Anthony, you play with matters of the heart as though they were mere trifles," Charlotte countered, her tone a delicate balance of doubt and longing.

Anthony, undeterred, closed the distance between them. "I confess my earlier intentions were misguided. My jests were a attempt to shield my heart from the vulnerability of genuine affection. But as I stand before you now, I cast aside the pretence. I cannot live without you,

Charlotte. I love you and want to marry you as soon as it can be arranged."

Her breath caught sharply in her throat. Dare she believe him and live happily ever after with him while fulfilling her duty to her family? Dare she?

"I do not need your dowry. Apart from my inheritance, I am wealthy in my own right. What people speculate as travelling to different countries to cavort with women is actually me pursuing various business interests which have made me a wealthy man. To prove to you that I want you and you alone, I don't require a dowry for our wedding...if you accept me. I want you to come to me just as you are."

Such beautiful words brought tears to her eyes, and a renewed hope to her heart.

"I went to the ball that day seeking a bride to put my mother's heart to rest, and fate brought you to me in the arbour. What joy I felt that night, but I had to hide it when I sensed your immense displeasure. Again, my insecurities came up, but I swore I would not allow them to deprive me of having you in my life again. Say you can forgive me for my folly and accept back the beautiful courtship we have shared these past weeks."

Noises of glee from her sisters who were discreet witnesses made her turn to them. She smiled when their heads bobbed eagerly, urging her to accept him.

As Anthony descended gracefully onto one knee, the murmurs of the onlookers, and the genteel rustle of gowns, all faded as Anthony made his heartfelt declaration.

"Lady Charlotte Norrington," Anthony intoned, his voice carrying the weight of sincerity and unspoken vows, "will you do me the honour of becoming my wife?"

Her eyes, pools of emotion, locked with his powerful gaze. A collective gasp rippled through the spectators as Charlotte, with a grace befitting a regal queen, offered her hand to Anthony.

"Yes, I'll marry you."

The crowd, previously enchanted by the spectacle, erupted into a chorus of delighted whispers and congratulatory murmurs. Her sisters clapped with excitement.

DAISY LANDISH

Anthony took her hand, kissed it, and rose with a wide grin across his face. The onlookers, caught in the rapture of the unexpected romance, erupted into another round of applause. Her sisters, their faces aglow with delight, rushed forward to envelop her in joyous embraces.

As the applause subsided, Charlotte and Anthony stood hand in hand, smiling into each other's eyes.

"I shall spend the rest of my life proving to you how much I love you," he declared with firmness.

"And I shall hold you to it, every day."

He chuckled.

"And by the way, I love you, too."

His answer was a sharp bark of laughter.

Epilogue

The wedding day dawned with an ethereal glow as if the universe itself acknowledged the sacred union taking place in the heart of England's countryside. A pristine chapel, adorned with cascading blossoms and flickering candles, stood witness to the culmination of Charlotte and Anthony's tumultuous journey to love.

Charlotte, resplendent in a gown of ivory silk and delicate lace, radiated a serene beauty that transcended the material trappings of nobility. The intricate embroidery, a testament to the meticulous craftsmanship of skilled artisans, adorned her figure like a cascade of moonlit stars. The cathedral-length veil, delicately trailing behind her, whispered promises of enchantment.

Anthony made a dashing figure in a tailored black coat, its richness accentuated by subtle gold embroidery. A pristine cravat framed his neck, an emblem of refined elegance, while a boutonnière of white roses nestled against the lapel.

The chapel, bathed in the soft glow of morning light, echoed with the hushed anticipation of a congregation eager to witness the union of two hearts. The air was tinged with the heady fragrance of lilies and roses.

As Charlotte approached the altar, a symphony of whispers rippled through the assembled guests. The delicate train of her gown, carried by her two sisters, seemed to float on air as she ascended the marble steps. Anthony, his gaze unwavering, stood at the altar, a portrait of quiet strength and anticipation.

The ceremony unfolded, steeped in regal tradition and solemnity. Vows exchanged, rings bestowed, and the sacred union sealed with a tender kiss; Charlotte and Anthony embarked on a new chapter as husband and wife.

Following the nuptials, the newlyweds retreated to the opulent Banbury estate, where a grand reception awaited. The ancestral home, adorned with sumptuous tapestries and glittering chandeliers, bore witness to the joyous celebration of their love.

Amidst the swirl of ballroom dances and clinking crystal, Charlotte and Anthony stole a moment of respite in the estate's enchanting garden. A hidden alcove, adorned with climbing roses and overlooking a tranquil pond, provided the perfect sanctuary for the couple to share the quietude of their newlywed bliss.

"Anthony," Charlotte began, her eyes sparkling with the effulgence of happiness.

"Yes, my duchess?"

She beamed with delight at his response and had to force herself not to get side-tracked. She needed to know the answer to what had disturbed her peace these past two years. "There's something I must know. Why did you propose a courtship with me, and then I find you in the arms of another woman hours later?"

Anthony took a deep breath before revealing the truth that had lingered as a shadow between them. "I had a change of heart because I feared you were too young for me. I feared that you wouldn't accept my proposal of marriage when a man with a loftier position and wealth came along. Remember, I wasn't a duke then, and I didn't have the means to provide for you."

Tears glistened in her eyes. "I didn't care about such things. Just like you, I fell in love with you at first sight and nothing else would have mattered to me except the love we shared."

He sighed. "If only I had known."

She sniffed. "Was that why you sought another woman?"

He hastily shook his head. "She threw herself at me. Stunned because she had never given any indication in the past as to favour me, I just stood there in shock until I realised I had to put an end to it. It was not my intention to hurt you, and I regretted it the moment it happened."

"I didn't know," she whispered in pain. "I thought you were merely toying with me. My friends laughed me to scorn, which made me so furious with you that I spread lies about you."

"I was foolish, Charlotte," Anthony continued, his voice a whisper of remorse. "I let fear dictate my actions, and in doing so, I hurt the one person I cherished most. I left, thinking it was the right thing for you. But I couldn't forget you, not for a single day."

She clasped his hand tightly. "Anthony, we both made mistakes. What matters is that we found our way back to each other. I believe in second chances, and I believe in us."

In that verdant alcove, where blossoms whispered secrets and the soft rustle of leaves bore witness to a love rekindled, Charlotte and Anthony sealed their commitment anew with a kiss.

The reluctant debutante had found not only love, but also a promise fulfilled under the gaze of a thousand stars.

The End

Charming The Lady

CLEAN REGENCY ROMANCE

Chapter One

The ballroom was a shimmering sea of silk and satin, a symphony of laughter and music. Lady Amelia Norrington, a vision of loveliness in her gown of ivory silk, moved gracefully across the dance floor, her blonde curls bouncing in rhythm with the music. Her ocean-blue eyes sparkled with delight as she twirled in her partner's arms, a handsome young earl.

Amelia was in her first season, and it had been a resounding success. She was one of the most sought-after debutantes in London. Her dance card, a delicate parchment adorned with intricate lettering, was always filled with the names of eager suitors, and her admirers were many, which was a testament to her popularity. Among them was the Duke of Wentworth, a wealthy and powerful man who had made no secret of his interest in her. His attention flattered her, and she found herself drawn to his charm and intelligence.

On the sidelines, her circle of friends watched with a mixture of admiration and envy. She heard them talking about her and smiled as her companion twirled her towards them.

With her auburn curls and piercing green eyes, Clara leaned in to talk to Elizabeth, a brunette with a sharp wit.

"Did you see the way Lord Turnstone looked at her? It's as if she's the only lady in the room," Clara remarked, her tone tinged with jealousy.

Elizabeth rolled her eyes, though a hint of a smile played on her lips. "Sweet Mary, Amelia has the entire *ton* at her feet. She's practically drowning in suitors."

Across the room, Amelia concluded her dance with a graceful curtsy. She approached her friends, noting how their faces were flushed with excitement, and their eyes held a hint of envy. As her suitor departed to fetch her refreshments, she joined them, the warmth of the dance still lingering in her cheeks.

"Amelia, you're positively radiant tonight," gushed Anne, a fair-haired beauty.

"You are simply divine tonight!" exclaimed Elizabeth, her voice dripping with admiration.

Amelia laughed softly. "Nonsense, ladies. We're all radiant and divine in our own ways."

"You have all the gentlemen swooning at your feet," Elizabeth added, her brown eyes sparkling with jealousy.

Amelia smiled graciously, trying to downplay the attention. "Oh, don't be silly. You all have plenty of suitors of your own."

Clara sighed wistfully. "But I'll wager none as handsome or wealthy as the Duke of Wentworth. You must tell us all your secrets. How did you capture his attention?"

Amelia's eyes twinkled mischievously. "Ah, the duke. He is charming, isn't he? But a lady must keep some secrets. Perhaps it's the mystery that intrigues him."

But her friends knew better. Amelia was the belle of the ball, and everyone knew it. She was beautiful, intelligent, and witty, and she had a way of making everyone feel special. Her oval face, ocean blue eyes, pert nose, pouting lips, gleaming blonde hair, and slightly curvy figure drew men like moths to a flame.

Amelia's gaze drifted to the Duke of Wentworth, who was watching her from across the room. He smiled at her, and she felt a flutter of excitement in her stomach.

Could he be the one? she wondered.

The thought was both thrilling and a little bit frightening. She had never been in love before and felt like something was missing. Of course, he would be considered as the perfect match for her with her being the second daughter of the late Duke of Ravenswood, but she couldn't help feeling as if there should be more.

The music started up again, and Amelia was whisked away to dance with another partner, a charming viscount with polished manners and a flattering smile. But her mind was still on the Duke of Wentworth. She couldn't help but glance at him now and then, and each time their eyes met, he smiled at her.

After the dance, Amelia went to stand by the punch bowl, chatting with a group of other debutantes. She was still on a high from the evening's events, and she couldn't help but feel a sense of anticipation for what the future held.

"Oh, my, he is coming."

Amelia looked in the direction of her friend's gaze and her breath caught in her throat as she saw the dashing Duke of Wentworth heading their way with a charming smile on his handsome face.

"May I have the honour of this dance?" he asked, extending his hand.

Amelia's heart fluttered, and she accepted his invitation without hesitation. They took to the dance floor, and she forgot about everything else in the world for a few blissful moments.

They danced together to the admiration of their spectators. As she twirled gracefully in her partner's arms, her laughter mingling with the lively strains of the orchestra, her attention was drawn to a tall, imposing figure standing amidst the throng of bystanders. Dressed in impeccably tailored black clothes, his dark brown hair swept back from his forehead, his piercing eyes seemed to follow her every move, an intense gaze that sent shivers down her spine.

She glanced away, dismissing it as a mere coincidence, but as she returned to her conversation with the duke, she couldn't shake the feeling that she was being watched. Time and again, her eyes would drift towards the mysterious stranger, only to find him fixedly observing her, his expression unreadable. A sense of unease settled over her, a prickling sensation that something was amiss.

The dance finally ended.

"May I call on you tomorrow?" the duke asked, his eyes filled with admiration.

Amelia blushed and nodded. "I would like that very much."

He smiled and kissed her gloved hand. "Until then," he said and disappeared into the crowd.

Amelia watched him go, her heart pounding in her chest. Was he going to be her future husband? Only time would tell.

She sought the company of her friends. Suddenly, she remembered the enigmatic stranger, hoping someone might recognise him. However, her queries were met with puzzled expressions and shrugs of uncertainty. *Can they not see him?* she wondered. Her apprehension grew, the lingering glances of the stranger casting a shadow over her otherwise joyous evening.

As the night progressed, Amelia found herself unable to ignore the stranger's persistent presence. Every time she turned a corner and paused to admire a piece of décor, his silhouette emerged from the crowd, his eyes locked on her, unwavering and unsettling. His silent scrutiny made her feel exposed and self-conscious as if her deepest secrets were being laid bare.

Despite her growing discomfort, she couldn't resist the urge to steal glances at him. His aura of mystery was both captivating and unnerving, his inscrutable presence drawing her like a moth to a flame.

After returning from the retiring room, she found herself face-to-face with the stranger. His eyes, deep pools of dark brown, bored into hers, sending a jolt of electricity through her veins. He was even more handsome up close. His square face, dark brown eyes, aquiline nose, firm lips, and clean-shaven jaw mesmerised her.

She opened her mouth to speak, but no words came out. He smiled, a faint curve of his lips, and then he was gone, disappearing into the night's embrace.

Amelia stood there, her heart pounding like a drum, her mind reeling from the encounter. His powerful presence had left an indelible mark on her, a lingering sense of foreboding that mingled with a strange, tingling anticipation.

Chapter Two

Two nights later, Amelia's heart pounded in her chest as she gazed across the crowded ballroom, searching for the mysterious stranger who had captured her attention. Her eyes scanned the sea of faces, hoping to catch a glimpse of his dark hair and piercing dark brown eyes.

Just as she was about to give up, she spotted him standing near the edge of the dance floor. He was even more striking than the other night; his tall, muscular frame in black clothes and white cravat commanding attention. She wondered if he would watch her again tonight, and she wasn't disappointed. His dark brown eyes fixed keenly on her a few minutes later as she conversed with her friends.

Every time she turned her head, his gaze seemed to intensify. The handsome stranger remained elusive, a shadow in the periphery of the glittering ballroom. Determined to unravel the mystery, she excused herself from her friends. She navigated the sea of dancing couples, her heart pounding with a mix of curiosity and apprehension. As she approached the pillars, the mysterious stranger stepped out of the shadows, revealing himself in the soft glow of candlelight. His dark brown eyes held a depth of intensity that set her pulse racing.

Amelia, undeterred by the air of mystery surrounding him, greeted him with a polite nod. "Good evening, my lord. May I inquire why you find me so fascinating?"

With a half-smile that hinted at a concealed secret, he replied in a smooth voice, "Good evening, Lady Amelia."

She gasped. *He knows who I am.*

"It is your breathtaking beauty, of course."

She blushed fierily. "You have me at a disadvantage, my lord. You know my name, but I do not know yours."

He bowed slightly. "Permit me to introduce myself, my lady. I am Jonathan Billsworth, the Marquess of Lennox."

Before she could reply, she found herself standing alone as the marquess withdrew into the shadows again. Unexpectedly, her friends, including the Duke of Wentworth, approached with inquisitive expressions.

"Amelia, who was that man?" Clara asked, her eyes wide with curiosity.

"I've never seen him before," Elizabeth added, casting a sceptical glance towards the departing marquess.

Amelia, her mind a whirlwind of emotions, struggled to find the right words. "He's the Marquess of Lennox."

The Duke of Wentworth frowned. "Lady Amelia, be cautious. The *ton* speaks of him as bad company. It would be wise not to associate with him."

Amelia, torn between the warnings of society and the intrigue the marquess had ignited within her, nodded in silent acknowledgement. Yet, the allure of the unknown proved irresistible. As the ball continued, she discreetly sought information about the marquess, but the *ton* remained tight-lipped, their whispers painting him as a shadowy figure with a past best left undisturbed.

It disappointed her that the one man she had found quite intriguing was elusive and believed to be a blackguard. However, when he approached her again by the punch bowl, ignoring the censorious eyes of the crowd as she conversed with a group of suitors, she held her breath.

"May I have this dance?" he asked, a charming smile playing on his lips. The ballroom hushed into a collective murmur as he extended a gloved hand towards her.

Should I accept? Should I? She remembered all the warnings she had received, but for the life of her, she desperately wanted to know more about him.

Amelia nodded shyly, her hand trembling as she accepted his outstretched arm. As her hand rested on his, she felt a spark of electricity course through her body. A wave of excitement swept over her as he led her to the dance floor. The eyes of the assembly followed them, whispers rippling through the room like a soft breeze. The dance commenced, and the couple moved with a grace that seemed to transcend the music itself.

Amelia's heart raced not just from the elegant dance, but from the electric connection she felt with him. His touch was firm yet gentle, and his eyes held a magnetic allure that drew her in.

As they moved across the floor, the atmosphere around them seemed charged with an unspoken tension. The gazes of the observers intensified, fuelled by curiosity and speculation.

"You dance divinely, Lady Amelia," the marquess whispered, his voice a velvety undertone that sent shivers down her spine.

"Thank you, my lord," she replied, her eyes searching his for answers, but she found none.

As the dance reached its crescendo, he spun her in a graceful twirl. The ballroom seemed to fade away, leaving only the two of them in a world of their own.

Amelia, determined to unravel the enigma the marquess was, spoke with a mix of curiosity and caution. "Why does the *ton* speak of you with such suspicion? What shadows do you carry, my lord?"

His expression remained unreadable. "In due time, Lady Amelia. Some truths are meant to unfold gradually. Patience is a virtue we both must embrace."

The dance continued, a silent dialogue unfolding between them. Amelia pressed for answers, and the marquess remained elusive, his words leaving her with more questions than before.

As the final notes of the music hung in the air, he halted their dance with a flourish. His dark eyes locked onto hers, and a promise lingered in the unspoken words that passed between them.

As the dance drew to a close, Amelia gathered her courage and asked him about his mysterious presence at the previous ball.

"I couldn't help but be drawn to you," he admitted, his eyes softening as he gazed at her. "There's something about you, Amelia, that makes me feel...alive."

Amelia blushed, her heart leaping with joy. Was it possible that he felt the connection, too? But he became evasive when she pressed him for more information about his past. He changed the subject, deflecting her questions with a practised finesse that only fuelled her curiosity.

Amelia was intrigued by his secrecy, and she couldn't deny the powerful attraction she felt towards him. She was determined to unravel the mystery that surrounded him, to discover the man behind the captivating façade.

The final strains of the waltz echoed through the ballroom as the marquess led Amelia into a graceful concluding bow, leaving her longing for more. The whispers of the *ton* intensified, swirling around the mysterious pair like a tempest.

"Lady Amelia," he declared, his voice carrying a weight of determination, "before the season is over, I shall make you mine."

With that bold proclamation, he bowed once more and vanished into the depths of the ballroom, leaving Amelia standing alone, her heart entangled in the mysterious promises of a man deemed unworthy by society.

Chapter Three

"Oh, you should have seen him, Sophia." Amelia twirled the skirts of her yellow muslin dress around her bedchamber the following morning. "He is incredibly handsome and charming. He told me he would make me his before the season ended."

Sophia, her sixteen-year-old sister, rolled her eyes as she put aside the book she was reading to stare at her sister. "Can't you speak of anything else besides the marquess?"

Amelia blinked and then smiled. "You'll understand when you become a debutante."

Sophia shivered perceptibly. "I am not looking forward to it."

Amelia giggled. "You can't read your way through life. You have to get married and have a family, eventually."

Sophia rolled her eyes again. "Please don't remind me."

Amelia laughed softly as her thoughts again went to the Marquess of Lennox.

"And what about the Duke of Wentworth?"

Amelia frowned. "What about him?"

"You hardly talked of anything else when he showed his interest in you. And now, it's the Marquess of Lennox. Do not make me think you're a fickle henwit like your friends."

A thick blush covered her face. "It is not like that, Sophia." She flounced on her bed. "I suspected something was missing with the duke, but with the marquess, it is there. I cannot say what it is precisely, but I feel it."

"I do not think Mother will like that you are passing on marrying a duke for a marquess," Sophia pointed out.

Amelia groaned inwardly. Duke Wentworth would be her mother's preferred choice because of his wealth and influence.

Chewing on her bottom lip, she strode to the windows, where sunlight streamed through the lace curtains. She was lost in her thoughts when her mother entered the room. Amelia whirled around as Sophia exited as their mother instructed her to.

Lady Elizabeth Norrington, a woman of impeccable grace and societal decorum, wore a stern expression that hinted at disapproval.

"Amelia, my dear," her mother began, her tone measured, "I must insist that you refrain from entertaining the Marquess of Lennox's advances. I have just learned of his true nature. He is a blackguard, a no-good pirate. You are to have nothing to do with him."

Amelia was stunned. She had heard whispers about Jonathan's past, but she had never imagined anything so scandalous. Her heart throbbed with pain, her dreams of a future with him shattering like glass. Her heart sank at the revelation. The man who had ignited a spark within her, who had promised to make her his before the season's end, was now tainted with an unsavoury reputation.

"But, Mother," she protested, her voice trembling.

"No, Amelia. He is not a perfect match for you," her mother exclaimed, her voice echoing through the room. "He has a reputation as a rogue, a philanderer, and a gambler. He is not fit for polite society, and I will not have you associate with him and ruin your reputation, and your chances with Duke Wentworth."

"Mother, what if they are wrong about him?" she asked frantically. "I spoke with him. He is not a rogue! Please listen to me, Mother."

The Dowager Duchess dismissed her daughter's pleas with a wave of her hand and walked over to her to place her arm around her shoulders. "You're too young to understand, Amelia," she said gently. "Men like that are nothing but trouble. They will use you and then discard you without a second thought. I forbid you ever to see him again. Focus your attention on His Grace. Do you hear me?"

She nodded solemnly, concealing the disappointment that welled within her. "Yes, Mother. I shall heed your warning."

After caressing her cheek, she exited the room, leaving Amelia alone with the shattered fragments of her burgeoning infatuation. As she gazed out of the window, a mix of sadness and longing enveloped her, for the mysterious marquess had become a forbidden dream.

In an attempt to escape the suffocating walls of her home, Amelia decided to take a walk in the garden. She summoned her maid, Margaret, a loyal companion who had been with her since childhood, to accompany her.

As Amelia strolled along the street, shielding her face from the sun's rays with her parasol, she couldn't keep thoughts of Jonathan from her mind. She knew too well about scandals to want to be associated with one. After seeing what it did to her older sister, Charlotte, she did not want to be a partaker, but she could not get the thought of the handsome man from her mind.

As if she conjured him, an opulent-looking large chaise stopped before her and the familiar silhouette that stirred both excitement and trepidation within her alighted from it. Jonathan, with an air of confidence that defied societal judgments, towered over her. Today, he was not dressed in his usual all-black clothing. He had on a brown coat, a snowy white shirt, and biscuit brown trousers.

"Good day, Lady Amelia," he greeted quietly.

Amelia, torn between her mother's warning and the undeniable pull of the handsome man, offered him a hesitant smile. "My lord, I must confess, I've been instructed to avoid your company."

He chuckled, falling into step with her. "Ah, the whispers of society. Lady Amelia, do not let the judgments of others dictate the desires of your heart. Gossip is a fickle companion."

Amelia, captivated by the sincerity in his gaze, questioned him. "Why is your reputation so tarnished? What truth lies behind the whispers?"

He sighed, his gaze momentarily distant. "I have lived a life that defies the expectations of society. A past that, though coloured by shadows, has shaped me into the man I am today. But let us not dwell on the judgments of yesterday."

"But..."

He fixed his mesmerizing eyes on her, and she was lost for words. "I wish to know more about you, Amelia. May I call you Amelia?"

It was wrong, but she did not mind.

"You can call me Jonathan," he added when she hesitated, and her eyes widened.

"I have found formalities a terrible bore."

She nodded. "I do, too."

"Very well, then. Amelia, tell me about your family. Begin with your father. I was sorry to learn that he is deceased."

Amelia hesitated, unsure if she should share such personal information with a man she hardly knew. But something about Jonathan's gentle demeanour and sincere interest put her at ease.

"I was not close to my father, so I cannot speak much about him. William, my older brother, acts like a father to us now." Her face lifted with a dazzling smile. "Charlotte, my older sister, is divine. I miss her terribly. She married the Duke of Banbury this year past, and they have been so happy together. She wrote to me recently that they are expecting their first child. I was so joyous."

Jonathan listened attentively, his eyes filled with admiration as she told him about her mother and younger sister.

"You have a wonderful family. Consider yourself fortunate to have them."

Amelia felt a surge of warmth towards him, grateful for his kind words. They fell into an easy conversation, their voices hushed as they strolled through the sun-streaked streets with passers-by staring at them. With gentle urging, she got him to talk. He spoke of his travels, his adventures, and his dreams for the future. She listened intently, captivated by his stories of his journeys to other countries and his infectious enthusiasm.

Despite her mother's warnings, she found herself falling for Jonathan's charm. She couldn't deny the powerful attraction she felt towards him.

Before parting ways, he looked at her with an intensity that made her heart race. "Amelia, you are unlike any other lady I've known. Trust your heart, not the gossip that seeks to cage it."

With those words, he bid her farewell, returning to his parked chaise. Amelia, left alone with the echoes of his presence, grappled with conflicting emotions. The warnings of her mother and the rumours about him clashed with the magnetic pull she felt toward him.

Amelia walked back to the house, her heart pounding with excitement. She knew that her increasing interest in Jonathan was forbidden, that she was risking everything by continuing to see him. But she couldn't deny the powerful magnetism she felt towards him, a pull that transcended all obstacles.

Chapter Four

As the days went by, Amelia's thoughts were consumed by Jonathan. His parting words echoed in her mind, leaving her uncertain about their future. Was she merely a distraction, a passing amusement to him, or did he mean to court her and marry her?

When she encountered the Duke of Wentworth at a musical and Venetian breakfast, he repeatedly asked to call on her but she stalled him because she was confused. Other gentlemen also asked for permission to court her, but she turned them down with the hope that Jonathan would approach her soon.

The upcoming ball of the season, the Duke and Duchess of Harcourt ball, loomed on Amelia's mind, a night filled with anticipation and uncertainty. She longed to see Jonathan again, to feel the warmth of his presence and the intoxicating rush of his charm. Yet, she couldn't ignore her mother's warnings and the disapproving whispers that followed Jonathan's name.

The day finally came, and Amelia donned her best dress yet. A pink satin dress with long sleeves, a round neckline, a full skirt with white lace trimmings on the hem, and big white bows at the waistline and shoulders. Pearls adorned her neck and ears, and her blonde hair was piled at the top of her head, with tendrils framing her beautiful face.

"I dare say His Grace will ask for your hand in marriage today with you looking so beautiful," her mother said as they rode in the chaise to the ball.

Amelia kept mute, for her mother did not know that she had been evading the duke's advances since the night she danced with Jonathan.

As the music filled the ballroom, Amelia scanned the crowd, her heart sinking with each passing moment. Jonathan was nowhere to be seen. The night grew dimmer, the laughter and chatter a dull backdrop to her mounting disappointment. Just as she was about to succumb to despair, the butler announced the Marquess of Lennox. Her breath caught in her throat as she watched him descend the winding stairs, a dashing figure in a burgundy coat, cream shirt, white cravat, black trousers, and shiny shoes. His tall, imposing frame stood out amidst the sea of dancers, his dark eyes scanning the room until they met hers. A mischievous smile played on his lips as he made his way towards her, his every step sending a jolt of electricity through her veins.

A murmur swept through the assembled guests as he approached her with a determined stride. Despite the disapproving glances that followed him, he had eyes only for her.

"You look stunning, my lady. A delightful vision in pink. You put other ladies to shame."

Her cheeks flushed as he extended his gloved hand to her, a silent invitation for a dance.

Amelia hesitated, her eyes flickering toward her mother standing a short distance away, whose stern expression mirrored the disapproval of the *ton*. Ignoring the collective frowning gaze, she placed her hand on Jonathan's, and they strode to the dance floor.

Despite the stern stares and hushed whispers that followed in their wake, their bodies moved in unison, their attraction a palpable force that defied the scrutiny of society. Amelia felt a surge of defiance, a determination to follow her heart, regardless of the consequences. She felt giddy with joy.

"Did you miss me?" he questioned with a grin.

She laughed softly. "What do you think?"

He smiled. "I think you missed me as much as I missed you."

Her heart skipped a beat. "Then why did you not seek me out?"

"I had pressing matters to attend to."

Amelia was a little disappointed that he did not think her important enough to seek her company these past few days.

"Tell me, Amelia, did your father say anything before he died?"

"Why are you so interested in my father?" she inquired, her eyes searching his for answers.

With a hint of melancholy in his gaze, he replied, "I knew your father before his demise. We met in the colonies."

She gasped. "You did?"

He nodded. "He was a gambler. As fate would have it, in a card game over there, he lost everything, including his estates, to a bet. And that *everything* now belongs to *me*."

Stunned by the revelation, Amelia felt the world around her crumble. "You're lying!" she exclaimed, her voice barely above a whisper.

Jonathan twirled her off the dance floor to a secluded spot beside the pillars. He reached into his pocket and pulled out a worn piece of parchment. "I hold in my possession the agreement your father signed, a pact that binds his losses to my gains. And there is another clause, Amelia. He wagered not just his estates, but also the hand in marriage of any of his daughters."

Amelia's stomach dropped as she recognized her father's signature, scrawled across the page in his familiar, elegant handwriting.

"It is fake," she remarked, her voice trembling with emotion. "My father would never agree to such a preposterous arrangement," she added, even though she knew it to be true.

Unfazed by her disbelief, he replaced the document in his pocket. "Believe what you will, Amelia, but the truth remains. Your father owed me a considerable sum of money, and he gambled his entire estate, including his daughters, to settle the debt."

Her mind whirled with confusion and disbelief as she realised his true motive for pursuing her. The man she had grown to love, the man who had captured her heart with his charm, was nothing more than a ruthless gambler.

"It is true, is it not? That you are a blackguard, a pirate! Mother was right. I should never have given you an audience."

He shrugged. "I merely seek to take what is mine. I would have approached your brother and laid the terms bare, but given that he is not in the country, I had to use whatever means necessary."

Amelia's heart sank. She couldn't believe that her own father would gamble away her future, her happiness, with such reckless abandon.

Without a word, she turned and fled the ballroom, her mind consumed by fear and uncertainty, leaving behind a sea of bewildered audiences.

Chapter Five

Amelia tossed and turned all night, her mind restless and tormented. Sleep eluded her, and the ticking of the clock in her chamber seemed to echo the relentless passage of time. Jonathan's revelation had shattered her illusions, revealing the dark truth behind his charming façade. She could hardly fathom how the man she had thought she had had a connection with could be so deceitful, so ruthless. Yet, the evidence was undeniable, the signed agreement hanging over her like a dark cloud.

As the first rays of dawn crept through her window, she rose, her body weary but her mind alert. After Margaret helped her with her ablutions, she made her way to her mother's room attired in a simple sky-blue morning dress, her heart pounding with anticipation.

After she fled from the ballroom the previous night to the garden, her mother had sought her out and blistered her ears for defying her and dancing with Jonathan. The dowager duchess had come down with a serious headache, and they had left the ball shortly after that. Her mother had taken ill and was still abed.

Amelia hesitated at the door, not wanting to disturb her mother in her fragile state, but she needed to know. She couldn't bear the weight of this secret any longer. She needed guidance. She knocked softly on the thick wooden door and opened it.

Her mother sat by the fireplace with a brown shawl draped over her shoulders. The subtle frailty in her appearance only heightened Amelia's sense of responsibility.

"Mother, how do you feel?" Amelia asked as she drew abreast, staring at the pale face of the woman she got her beauty from.

"I am feeling much better this morning, my dear," she replied in a light tone.

"Mother, I must apologise for disobeying you last night. If only I had known better."

A frown contorted the older woman's face. "Amelia, my dear, did something happen between you and the despicable marquess? I could not help noticing how silent you were on the ride back, even though I was feeling out of sorts then."

The cough that left her mother's lips after her words of concern made Amelia hesitate in telling her what transpired between her and Jonathan. She had come to the room to reveal everything, but after seeing her mother's sick state, she did not want to add to her distress.

"Mother," she began, her voice barely above a whisper as she evaded her question. "There is something I must ask you."

"What troubles you, my dear?"

Amelia took a deep breath, summoning the strength to voice the questions that lingered in the shadows of her mind. "Father returned from America shortly before he fell ill, did he not?"

Her mother nodded solemnly. "Yes."

Amelia's brow furrowed. "Was he a gambler?"

She inhaled sharply. "Who told you that?"

"It does not matter. Please answer me, Mother."

She sighed and leaned back in her chair. "Yes, he was. It was like a disease that could not be cured in him."

Tears stung Amelia's eyes because she had been hoping Jonathan's claims were false. "His gambling habits... they were the source of our family's troubles, were they not?"

She had heard they were in financial ruin but had not bothered much about it until it was Charlotte's first season. Then she had learnt that they all had to make good matches to secure the family's fortunes.

"Your father, despite his...virtues, had a weakness for games of chance. He engaged in high-stakes gambling, and the consequences proved disastrous. He nearly gambled us out of house and home."

He has! Oh, how she wished she could tell her what was going on. But would it not make her failing health deteriorate? She did not want to lose the sweet woman.

How I wish I never laid eyes on Jonathan! He had brought so much heartache and sorrow to her. To think she had envisaged marrying him when he was only out to ruin her family.

The shame and disgrace that hung over her family were the direct result of her father's vices. Yet, the burden of rectifying the situation now rested on her shoulders.

Her mother, sensing the turmoil within her, reached out to tenderly caress her cheek. "My dear, I would spare you this knowledge if I could. But the past cannot be changed. It is the present and the future that we must face."

Amelia nodded. "I understand, Mother."

"His gambling was not well known, which has saved us a lot of embarrassment. That is why I must ask you again to desist from accepting the marquess's advances. He is of disrepute. We do not want another scandal tied to our family's name, do we?"

She shook her head. Her heart ached at the sight of her mother's distress. She could not bear the thought of her family name being tarnished, their reputation ruined by her father's reckless actions.

"Splendid. The Duke of Wentworth is a good man, and he appears to be in love with you. Give him a chance. I believe he will make you happy. Inscrutable men like the marquess are best avoided, for they do not bode well for your future."

She nodded. "Very well, Mother. I shall heed your counsel."

Amelia decided not to disturb her ailing mother any further. Instead, she retreated to her own chambers, her mind racing with plans to navigate the treacherous waters that lay ahead.

The absence of her older sister and her brother heightened the sense of loneliness. She longed for Charlotte's wisdom, whose experience in navigating societal complexities could provide invaluable guidance. Charlotte had married and moved away, and William was pursuing business interests outside of London. In their absence, the burden of salvaging the family's honour fell squarely on her shoulders. Sophia always had her nose in a book to be of much help.

With a heavy heart, Amelia realized that she would have to face the challenges alone.

Chapter Six

The sun shone brightly overhead as Amelia alighted from the chaise in Hyde Park, a popular gathering spot for the upper echelons of society. Jonathan had told her that he frequented the park, seeking respite from the confines of his townhouse. There, amidst the serene trees and tranquil lakes, she hoped to find him and engage in a decisive conversation. The park, adorned with the hues of spring, offered her a temporary refuge from her solemn thoughts about her future.

As she strolled along the park's meandering paths with Margaret, her heart pounded with a mix of anxiety and anticipation. Every rustle of leaves in the breeze, every peal of distant laughter, sent a jolt of apprehension through her, knowing that Jonathan would likely seek her out. Suddenly, the sound of approaching footsteps caused her heart to thump in her chest. Even before she turned around, she knew it was him. The gentle breeze carried his cedar fragrance to her nostrils. She spotted him standing beneath the shade of an ancient oak tree. His dark brown hair glistened in the sunlight, his impressive frame casting a long shadow on the manicured lawn. Her breath caught in her throat as he approached her. His eyes met hers, his gaze unwavering, piercing through her soul. Despise him as she did, she could not deny that she found him incredibly handsome, and his presence sent bolts of awareness through her body like no man had ever done.

With a measured gaze, she turned fully to face him, her eyes reflecting defiance. "What is it that you want, my lord?"

He arched a brow. "No salutations?"

"You do not deserve one, my lord."

He gave her a stiff smile. "I thought we were on a first name basis."

"That is no longer the case as you have sought to ruin my family."

He sighed. "It is my right to claim what is duly mine, Amelia," he declared, his tone unyielding. "Your family's estates and properties are bound by the ink of the contract."

"How am I sure the contract is legally binding?"

He shrugged. "We could take it to a solicitor of your choice. I won the game fair and square. I have witnesses."

Amelia, though internally prepared for this moment, felt the weight of reality pressing upon her. "Then you must allow me to marry The Duke of Wentworth. He will gladly pay off my family's debts, and we can settle this matter without undue hardship."

He regarded her with a penetrating gaze, his expression unmoved. "You have him wrapped around your little finger, do you not?"

A blush crept up her face, and she looked away. "Unlike you, he has been very sincere with his pursuit."

"You think I was not sincere?"

"I know you only mean to see my family's ruin and humiliation when word gets out that you now own us."

"You misunderstand. I—"

She rapidly shook her head, releasing strands of her hair from the pins that held them through the act. She did not want him to know how hurt she was by his deceit. He would only laud it over her. "It does not matter. What do you say about my proposal of the duke paying you off?"

His brown eyes became darker. "You underestimate the gravity of your father's debts, Amelia. They are not easily appeased. The only way I would consider forgiving them and tearing this contract asunder is if you agree to marry me."

She recoiled at the proposition, her inner turmoil etched across her face. The gravity of the decision she faced loomed before her like an insurmountable mountain.

"But... marrying you would mean surrendering my intention to marry the duke," she protested, her voice tinged with reluctance, even though she had been stalling the duke because of Jonathan. How foolish of her now! She should have accepted his proposal to court her. She would have easily gone to him with her problems now.

"If you desire to become a duchess, then you will be one at my father's passing," he quietly told her.

Her face became inflamed with anger. "How dare you insinuate that I am a vain and vapid lady only interested in titles?"

He shrugged. "I had not thought so when we first met, but what else am I supposed to think by your statement?"

Too incensed to measure her words, she snapped, "I meant love, not that I expect you to know anything about it. I love the duke."

His eyes narrowed. "You have a funny way of showing it, given the way you eagerly welcomed my advances."

Her face reddened further. "I was merely punishing Edwin," she retorted using the duke's given name. Jonathan's brows furrowed. "We quarreled, and I wanted to show him I could easily get another man's interest." Her voice drifted to a whisper. "Unfortunately, I chose the devil's spawn to play my games with."

"Wise words," he replied with iciness. "Do not ever do that again. I am not a man to be trifled with."

Her heart clenched with pain. "That I know now." She lifted pleading eyes to his. "Would you not reconsider for the sake of love?"

With a calculated resolve, he responded, "Your family's honour hangs in the balance, Amelia. Sometimes, sacrifices must be made for the greater good."

A heavy silence settled between them, the weight of the decision palpable in the spring air. If she did not agree to his proposal, shame and disgrace would come to her family. She had to consider her mother and Sophia, who would need a good reputation to find a perfect match. Torn between duty and hatred for Jonathan for making her fall for him and then pulling the carpet from under her, she finally nodded with a sense of reluctant acceptance. "Very well, my lord. For the sake of my family's honour, I agree to your terms. But promise me this, once I marry you, you will release my family from the debt."

With a subtle nod, he acknowledged her plea. "I promise, Amelia. Once our union has served its purpose, your family will be free from the shadows of this contract."

With a solemn nod, he extended a gloved hand, and Amelia, with a heavy heart, placed hers in it. The leaves whispered their witness, the park bearing silent testimony to a union forged in the crucible of necessity. The looming prospect of marriage to a man she now loathed and did not trust became an inevitable fate.

She turned away, but he stopped her with his hand on her arm. "Perhaps we could take a stroll around the park."

She eyed him with suspicion. "Of what use would it be? There is no longer a need for pretence on your path, my lord."

Jonathan's eyes narrowed, his expression unreadable. "If we are to have a successful courtship and marriage, we must keep appearances... and remain friends."

She shook her head. "We were never friends, my lord. You were simply a moment of aberration on my part which I sorely regret now."

His lips thinned. "Very well. If that is the way you want it, so be it. I shall call upon you tomorrow."

With those clipped words, he walked away, leaving her heart in turmoil. Days ago, she would have been over the moon that Jonathan had asked for her hand in marriage, but now, all she felt was a hollowness that threatened to consume her. The weight of duty to her family seemed too much for her to bear, leaving her in despair.

Chapter Seven

News of Amelia's impending union with Jonathan sent shockwaves through the upper echelons of London society. Whispers of Jonathan's shady past and ruthless reputation spread like wildfire, casting a cloud of disapproval over the engagement.

Amelia was at the centre of a maelstrom of criticism and speculation. Her friends and acquaintances expressed their concerns, warning her of the dangers of associating with such a man. But Amelia, determined to honour her word and fulfil her duty to her family, remained steadfast in her decision. The Duke of Wentworth expressed his disapproval of her rejecting him using the vilest of words, which shocked her. Underneath his calm façade lay a man with deep anger issues, and she was glad she had not accepted his advances. However, his harsh words cut her like a knife.

She sought the cover of darkness, in search of solace in the quiet solitude of the gardens, away from prying and censorious eyes. The night air was cool and refreshing, and she wandered through the paths of the blossoming roses and manicured hedges.

As she rounded a bend, a figure emerged from the shadows, a familiar silhouette that stirred both excitement and trepidation within her. Jonathan towered over her, his eyes gleaming in the moonlight. Her heart skipped a beat, a mixture of wariness and excitement coursing through her.

"You should not be here," she whispered, her voice barely audible.

He smiled, a mischievous glint in his eyes. "And you should not be out here alone at night."

She blushed, embarrassed at her indiscretion. She felt shame for the thrill that shot through her at seeing him again, even after what he threatened to do to her family if she did not marry him.

"If my father did not recently tell me that Edwin and I are distantly related, I would have called him out for what he did to you in there," he remarked, stunning her that he had noticed her exchange with the duke even when he was standing across the ballroom.

She shrugged. "It does not matter. And he is not at fault."

He paused in his stride and his hand curled under her chin to lift it. "You defend a man who caused these tears in your beautiful eyes?"

She looked away. "He thinks I led him on. My acceptance of your proposal made him a laughingstock amongst his peers. Surely, you must understand how he feels."

"That does not give him the right to treat you in such a disdainful manner. If it were not that we share ancestry in some way, I would have put a bullet in his shoulder in a duel to teach him some manners."

Despite her wretchedness at the way society had ostracized and criticized her for her union with him, she could not help the smile that crossed her face.

"You merely jest. You will do no such thing."

His eyes held a promise that made her mouth run dry. "With time, you will come to know that I do not trifle with what is mine, and I do not allow anyone else to do such."

Her face contorted in a frown. "So, I am just a property to you?"

An expression flashed across his face that she could not understand. "Mayhap you will also come to know how much you mean to me soon."

Undeterred by his seemingly passionate words and the warmth that spread through her, she retorted, "I already do. Some thousands of pounds and everything my father owned before his death."

He winced. "I did not mean it that way."

She made to turn away, already regretting why she entertained a conversation with him, but he forestalled her with a hand on her bare arm.

"I am sorry, Amelia."

She eyed him with confusion. "'Tis not your fault. Father should have known better."

"I apologize for you losing the love of your life because of me."

A rosy hue covered Amelia's face as she recalled her fib to him about loving Edwin. She nodded.

"The ballroom is stifling. Would you mind walking with me for a little while?"

"But..." She trailed to a stop.

He grinned. "Are you wondering what the gossipy *ton* will say about us being alone together? You need not bother yourself, Amelia. I have realized that to worry about gossip is to cause yourself untold heartache." His smile widened. "Besides, we are already betrothed."

Before she could stop herself, she replied, "I do not remember you asking me to marry you. It was more of an ultimatum."

With his eyes twinkling with warmth, he said, "Allow me to remedy that, my lady."

Her eyes widened when he went down on one knee. "Lady Amelia Norrington, would you do me the honour of becoming my wife?"

Before she could respond, some people came out of the ballroom to interrupt them. Amelia, with her heart racing, turned and ran back into the ballroom, tears glistening in her eyes.

Her mother, initially unaware of what was going on because of her ill-health, eventually did when she became well. She forbade Amelia from further seeing Jonathan, and Amelia was forced to tell her the reason she accepted his proposal. She shared the details of her father's gambling debts and the binding agreement, revealing the depth of her sacrifice.

"Mother," Amelia said, her voice gentle yet resolute, "I need you to understand why I've chosen this path. It is not about my desires but about saving our family's name."

The dowager duchess turned to face her daughter, lines of weariness etched across her features. "I cannot bear to see you entangled with a man whose past is shrouded in shadows. Your father's mistakes should not dictate your future."

As her mother listened while Amelia explained further, her stern expression softened into one of heartbreak. The weight of the truth bore down on her and tears glistened in her eyes. "Oh, my dear Amelia, what has your father wrought upon us? I never imagined our family would be entangled in such a web of humiliation."

Amelia, her own eyes brimming with unshed tears, said, "Mother, I do this not for myself but for the honour of our family. I bear the weight willingly, for it is my choice."

Overcome with a mix of emotions, she embraced her daughter. "You are stronger than I ever imagined, Amelia. Putting family before your own desires is a testament to your character. I am proud of the lady you have become, just like Charlotte."

Amelia's heart swelled with gratitude for her mother's understanding and support.

"I have sent word to William for him to return to England posthaste. He will resolve the matter before the wedding."

Amelia merely nodded, for she did not think she could escape marrying Jonathan.

As the weeks of their courtship progressed, she found herself surprisingly drawn to Jonathan's charismatic charm and unconventional ways. Despite his reputation as a ruthless pirate, there was a flicker of kindness in his eyes, a hint of tenderness in his touch. His intelligence and wit captivated her, his adventurous spirit igniting a spark within her. Yet, she couldn't shake the lingering doubts that clouded her heart. She could not forget the cruel terms of their agreement, the way he had manipulated her desperation to save her family's reputation to secure her hand in marriage. She could not reconcile the man she was growing to love again with the ruthless pirate the *ton* so vehemently warned her about.

With each passing day, Amelia's conflicting emotions intensified. She was torn between her growing affection for Jonathan and the lingering doubts about his true character. She longed for happiness, for a life of love and companionship, but she feared that her union with him would only lead to heartbreak and despair.

Chapter Eight

Encouraged by Jonathan, Amelia decided to join the grand hunting party hosted by Lord and Lady Grisham in the picturesque countryside away from the incessant judgmental whispers. Amelia, still adjusting to her role as Jonathan's betrothed, found herself amidst a lively gathering of gentlemen and ladies who did not care about what the *ton* thought of them. Their laughter and chatter echoed through the opulent Grisham Manor.

Jonathan, in his element, led Amelia through the festivities, introducing her to their fellow guests and engaging in lively conversations. Amelia, initially overwhelmed by the sheer scale of the events, gradually warmed up to the company, her natural charm and grace winning over the hearts of those she met.

The sprawling countryside offered a canvas of vibrant colours, the russet leaves underfoot, the azure sky stretching above, and the verdant hills that rolled into the distance. Amelia, adorned in practical yet elegant riding attire, felt a sense of liberation.

The hunting party ventured deep into the woods, their laughter and camaraderie resounding through the trees. Jonathan, ever the daunting figure, demonstrated a proficiency with both horse and rifle that surprised Amelia. As they traversed the rough terrain together, a bond formed between them, unspoken connections woven through shared experiences.

Amelia revelled in the freedom that horseback riding offered. Jonathan, his eyes alight with a shared enthusiasm, matched her stride as they ventured into the heart of the wilderness. As the horses galloped through open fields, the rhythmic beat of hooves creating a symphony, Jonathan turned to Amelia with a playful glint in his eyes. "Shall we race, my lady?"

Amelia, her laughter carried away by the wind, met his challenge with a mischievous smile. "Very well, but no cheating this time."

The race commenced, the horses tearing through the open expanse with an exhilarating speed. The wind whistled in their ears. The crisp spring air invigorated Amelia as she galloped through the countryside, her laughter echoing across the rolling hills. Jonathan, on his sleek black stallion, kept pace beside her, his eyes sparkling with amusement.

"You're cheating!" she cried, her voice breathless but playful.

He threw back his head and laughed, his deep baritone rumbling through the air. "Nonsense! You simply lack my equestrian prowess."

In the end, Jonathan's horse crossed the finish line just ahead of Amelia's.

Laughing breathlessly, she accused him with mock indignation. "You cheated again! I demand a rematch."

Patting his horse's head with a grin, he feigned innocence. "Cheated, my lady? I assure you, I am a paragon of fair play."

Unconvinced but still smiling, she conceded the point. "Very well, my lord, a rematch it shall be. But no more underhanded tactics. I bet I can outrun you if we race to the creek."

He raised a brow, a mischievous glint in his eyes. "Challenge accepted, but I warn you, I will not go easy on you."

With a playful grin, Amelia dug her heels into the horse's flank. The chestnut gelding surged forward, his powerful muscles rippling beneath his sleek coat. The two horses became a blur of dark and brown against the lolling landscape.

Neck and neck they raced, the wind whipping through their hair, their laughter blending with the pounding hooves. Amelia felt alive, her spirit soaring with the freedom of the open countryside.

Just as the creek came into view, Jonathan leaned forward, his hair falling across his forehead, and crossed the finish line a hair's breadth before Amelia.

She pulled up, panting but grinning. "Fine, you win," she conceded.

Jonathan chuckled, dismounting with his usual grace. "Why, thank you, my lady."

They walked their horses down to the babbling creek, the sunlight dappling the water with a mosaic of light and shadow. Jonathan sat on a moss-covered rock, casting his line with practiced ease. Amelia watched him, admiring the way his muscles moved with fluid strength.

"You seem confident," she teased, picking up her own fishing rod. "I might just catch the biggest fish today."

He smirked. "We shall see about that, my braggart fiancé."

Amelia, a determined glint in her eyes, cast her line into the water. The stillness of the lake mirrored the quiet anticipation that settled between them. The hours melted away as they fished, the silence punctuated by the occasional splash of water and the chirping of crickets. Amelia's line grew taut, and she reeled in a wriggling sizeable trout, a triumphant grin plastered on her face.

"See?" she crowed, holding up her catch triumphantly. She turned to Jonathan with a boastful grin. "Look, my lord! A catch fit for a skilled angler such as myself. The creek favors the determined angler."

He examined the fish with mock seriousness. "Impressive," he conceded. "But I believe mine is a fighter."

He pulled his line, revealing a glistening perch, not quite as large as her trout. They compared their catches, their laughter resonating through the valley.

Jonathan, feigning awe, applauded her accomplishment. "Impressive, my lady. Clearly, your skills surpass even the most seasoned fishermen."

Basking in the glory of her triumph, she could not resist a playful jab. "Perhaps you would like a lesson. It seems you have much to learn in the art of fishing."

Jonathan, with a twinkle in his eyes, responded with a theatrical bow. "I humbly accept, Amelia. Teach me your ways, and I shall strive to become a master of the angler's craft."

She laughed heartily.

As the sun began its descent, casting long shadows across the water, they packed up their things, their hearts full of contentment. The day had been a simple one, a shared passion for the outdoors and each other's company. But in its simplicity, it held a profound beauty, a reminder of the joy found in the quiet moments, the shared laughter, and the attraction that bloomed under the open sky.

As they continued their week in the backwoods, the competition and banter between them forged a bond that transcended any obstacle. The echoes of laughter and shared victories carried them through the untouched beauty of nature.

As the days unfolded into a succession of adventures, from brisk rides across open fields to evenings in the gardens under the twinkling stars, Amelia found herself drawn to Jonathan, just like when they first met. Their conversations, once tinged with the weight of obligation, flowed effortlessly in the unguarded moments under the vast canopy of the sky. She marvelled at the shared interests they discovered; literature, a mutual appreciation for the arts, and a passion for the untamed beauty of the outdoors. She learned about Jonathan's experiences abroad, the places he had been, and the stories that had shaped him into the man she now knew him to be— a privateer and not a pirate as erroneously assumed by the *ton*.

In the quiet moments of reflection, Amelia could not deny the blossoming emotions within her. The realization struck her like a sudden gust of wind, a torrent of emotions she could not suppress. She was in love with Jonathan!

Yet, beneath the blossoming of her own emotions lay a twinge of sadness. The awareness that her love was unreciprocated, that the connection they shared might remain confined to the realm of friendship, cast a subtle shadow over the splendid days in the woods.

Chapter Nine

Their stay in the countryside came to an end, and Amelia and Jonathan returned to the bustling city of London. The social season was in full swing, and the grand townhouses were abuzz with excitement as the aristocracy gathered for balls, dinners, and soirées. As the hunting party dispersed, Amelia was once again enveloped in the familiar embrace of societal expectations and the shadows that clung to her association with Jonathan.

Amelia, adorned in a gown that matched the colour of her ocean blue eyes, descended the grand staircase to the family drawing room. She strode into the elegant room, decked with opulent furnishings and paintings. The familiar faces of her mother and brother awaited her, and in their eyes, she sensed a blend of curiosity and concern.

Her mother greeted her with an affectionate smile and hug. "Welcome back, my dear. How was the trip into the countryside?"

Amelia offered a diplomatic response, painting the journey with the hues of pleasant memories while skilfully sidestepping the complexities of her strengthening relationship with Jonathan. Her mother's perceptive gaze, however, hinted at an unspoken understanding.

She also hugged her brother, ignoring the questioning gaze in his blue eyes. "How was your trip, William?" she asked as she settled on the brocaded armchair by the French window.

"As well as can be expected."

"I have missed you."

He grinned, his handsome face softening. "As have I, my darling sister. After our discussion, I will present you with the gifts I procured for you."

"How delightful!"

An uneasy cloak of silence fell in the drawing room that stretched taut Amelia's nerves. She was more than certain that her mother had relayed to William all that had happened since his departure from England. She wondered what her older brother would say.

As the family, excluding Sophia, partook of afternoon tea, Amelia sensed her apprehension rising as her brother did not say anything about Jonathan but conversed about his travels.

"I have been apprised of the situation, Amelia," he finally said, his voice carrying the weight of responsibility. "Mother has informed me about the... arrangement you made with the Marquess of Lennox."

She met her brother's gaze, finding a mixture of pride and concern. "I did what I believed was necessary, William. Duty to the family name comes before personal desires."

He nodded approvingly, acknowledging the sacrifices she had made. "Your sense of duty does you credit, Amelia. However, I have news that may lighten the burden you have shouldered. I have accumulated enough wealth through my business endeavours these many months that I have been away. You need not be bound to the marquess any longer."

Her heart skipped a beat at the unexpected revelation. She looked at her brother with surprise. "You have made enough money to settle the debts?"

He offered a reassuring smile. "Indeed. The family's honour can be restored without the need for further entanglements with the marquess. You can be free from the forced betrothal."

Amelia's face paled at the news. She ought to be joyous that she would no longer be shackled by her father's debt to Jonathan, yet it felt as if it was the most terrible news she had ever received.

She darted her tongue across her lips, struggling to evade her mother's penetrating gaze. "You...you mean, he and I will no longer get married?"

Her brother nodded. "There will be no need for you to continue seeing him. We can resolve this matter without sacrificing your happiness. I shall summon him and tell him to name his price."

Grasping at straws because she could not imagine life without the man she had grown to love, she asked, "Would it not cause a scandal? The whole of England knows we are to be wed soon."

He shrugged. "From what I heard at White's and in the gossip mill, everyone would be relieved that you did not marry the blasted pirate. You need not worry about making a perfect match after breaking off the betrothal. With a huge dowry, any sensible man will forget that you were once engaged to the marquess."

Amelia, however, hesitated, her mind grappling with the unspoken complexities of her feelings. "Jonathan is not a pirate, as the rumours suggest. He is a privateer, and there is a distinction."

Her brother's eyebrows raised in surprise at her firm defence. "A privateer? It does not change anything."

Amelia took a steadying breath, her gaze meeting her brother's with a mixture of determination and vulnerability. "Jonathan has navigated treacherous waters, and I can't dismiss him based on society's judgments. There's more to him than meets the eye."

The room fell into a contemplative silence as William absorbed the nuances of his sister's words. Her mother, though initially reserved, spoke with a gentleness that belied her motherly concern. "Amelia, your heart is noble, but you need not sacrifice your happiness for the sake of duty. There are other ways to settle our debts." Peering keenly at her, she continued. "Is there a reason you hesitate to accept your brother's suggestion?"

How do I tell you that I have fallen in love with the man who callously threatened to ruin us and I desire to marry him?

Amelia, aware of the unspoken expectations, masked her true emotions beneath a facade of gratitude. "No reason, Mother." She turned to her brother. "Thank you, William. I appreciate your efforts, and I shall desist from further association with the marquess henceforth, and allow you to deal with him as you see fit."

"Brilliant!" William gave her a beatific smile.

"May I be excused?" She rose at her mother's nod and curtsied before leaving the room with a heavy heart.

With hurried steps, she went up to her room as she grappled with the conflicting paths that lay before her. The choice between duty and personal happiness. Her family would never accept a man who had forced her into a betrothal simply because her late father was indebted to him. Again, she was forced to choose between her family and her heart's desires.

Tears poured down her face at the realization that her liaison with Jonathan, the man she loved had come to an end. William's newfound financial prowess meant that they could finally settle Jonathan's debt, releasing Amelia from the binding agreement that had brought them together.

She yearned for Jonathan's companionship, his wit, his intelligence, and the way he made her feel alive. But she had to prepare herself for the inevitable goodbye. She smiled through her tears at the wonderful memories they shared when they were in the countryside. They would forever be inscribed in her heart.

She wished she could see him one more time, but there was no point in going to the dinner party with him the following night. She was certain William would have spoken to him by then and they would come to an arrangement. After all, it was not as if he loved her. Only the debt had kept them together. Her heart squeezed with the pain of unrequited love.

Chapter Ten

Tears again threatened to fall from Amelia's eyes as she stood by the windows, her gaze fixed on the manicured gardens beyond. The lingering scent of afternoon tea and the muted sunlight filtering through the heavy curtains created an ambiance of subdued grandeur.

William had shattered her world two days ago when he told her she would no longer need to bother herself about her betrothal to Jonathan. She had gone about with a smile on her face, but her heart had been held bound by despair.

All William had told her when he returned after his meeting with Jonathan was that it was settled and she would no longer have to bother herself about duty again. She had not known what it meant and neither had she wanted to ask for fear that Jonathan had agreed to take the money instead of insisting he wanted to marry her as she had secretly hoped.

The only good thing she supposed came out of the meeting was William telling her that he no longer believed that Jonathan was a pirate. But what good would that be to her when she had lost the man she loved?

She turned away from the window and walked up to the fireplace to stare at the portrait of her father on the mantle. If only he had not gambled away their fortune and made such a callous arrangement, she would never have met Jonathan and had her heart broken now.

From a faraway distance, she heard the front door slam shut and hurried footsteps headed her way. She whirled around with surprise when Jonathan thrust open the double doors of the room with the harried butler standing behind, trying to announce him before his entrance.

Jonathan shut the doors in the elderly man's face. He strode in with a purposeful gait. His dark eyes, usually guarded, revealed a vulnerability that mirrored the turmoil within her soul.

Amelia's heart leaped with surprise and anticipation. Jonathan's demeanour was uncharacteristically subdued, his normally confident gaze clouded with uncertainty.

As they settled into the drawing room, Jonathan's silence grew even more palpable. Amelia, sensing his inner turmoil, waited patiently for him to speak. Finally, he broke the silence, his voice barely a whisper.

"Amelia," he uttered, his voice carrying a weight that transcended the confines of social formalities. "There is something I must say, and I can no longer let it go unsaid."

Amelia turned to face him, her gaze meeting his with a mixture of anticipation and trepidation. The air in the room seemed to thicken as Jonathan took a step closer, his eyes searching hers with intensity.

"Amelia," he began, his eyes filled with a mix of vulnerability and determination, "I have come to realise that my feelings for you extend far beyond the terms of our agreement."

Amelia's breath caught in her throat, her heart pounding in her chest. Could this be what she had longed for, the reciprocation of her love, the declaration she had yearned to hear?

"What... what are you saying?" she asked, her voice trembling with emotion.

Jonathan, his expression filled with sincerity, smiled. "I am saying that I love you, Amelia," he declared, his voice resonating with conviction. "I love your intelligence, your spirit, your strength. I love the way you challenge me, and the way you make me feel alive."

Amelia's heart soared with joy, tears welling up in her eyes. The love she had silently harboured for Jonathan was being reciprocated, a validation that sent shivers of happiness down her spine.

"Oh, Jonathan," she whispered, her voice choked with emotion.

"I've realised that no amount of wealth or societal expectations can compare to the depth of what I feel for you. I do not care about the contract. I do not care about the money. My heart yearns for you. Only you."

The gravity of his words resonated within the drawing room, casting aside the shadows that had lingered for far too long. With a newfound resolve, she stepped forward, her eyes locked with his. "Jonathan," she began, her voice trembling with a vulnerability that mirrored his own, "I love you, too. More than societal norms and family obligations."

A tender smile graced Jonathan's lips as he reached out to gently cup her face. The warmth of his touch, a reassurance that transcended words, spoke of a connection that surpassed the constraints of societal expectations.

With a triumphant smile, he reached into his pocket and pulled out the contract, the binding agreement that had brought them together but also threatened to tear them apart. Without hesitation, he tore it into pieces, the fragments fluttering to the floor like confetti. The torn remnants of the contract fluttered to the floor, an emblem of liberation from the chains that bound them.

Amelia's heart swelled with gratitude as she watched Jonathan's symbolic gesture. He drew her into his arms and kissed her. She pulled away from him, her eyes gleaming with love and joy.

"I do not understand. William told me I would never have to worry about my duty to the family again."

He laughed softly. "That is because I told him how I felt about you, and that I no longer cared about the contract. As a matter of fact, from the moment I set my eyes on you, I stopped caring about the money."

She stared at him in disbelief. "But you said..."

"I know what I said, my love. I was afraid of losing you. I saw the way men flocked around you, especially Edwin, and I thought I did not stand a chance, particularly as my reputation is not stellar. My encounter with a pirate some years ago made the *ton* think that I was one. I never bothered to correct the impression because I did not care.

But for your sake, I will set the record straight with the help of the Royal Navy."

She shook her head. "I do not care what they think about you. I love you and you love me and that is all that matters."

He lowered his eyes. "You no longer love Edwin."

A giggle burst from her throat. "I never loved him. I used him as an excuse to hide my feelings for you because I was hurt that you were forcing me into marriage."

He cupped her cheek. "I am so sorry for hurting you, my love. My brothers told me it was a stupid idea to bring up the contract so soon, but I panicked and acted like a fool. Forgive me?"

She beamed. "But of course."

"We were interrupted last time when I wanted to declare my love to you in the form of a proposal." He went on a bended knee. "Will you marry me, love of my life?"

She nodded, beaming. "Yes, Jonathan. I will marry you."

He rose, smiling. "I look forward to going on multiple journeys with you," he said, drawing her into his arms again.

Smiling brightly, Amelia released a heavy sigh. Her season of intrigue had ended with her finding a man she would cherish for the rest of her life.

The End

Defying The Lady
CLEAN REGENCY ROMANCE

Chapter One

The flickering glow of candlelight cast a warm ambiance in the Duke of Ravenswood's study, where heavy velvet curtains adorned the windows and shelves lined with leather-bound tomes stretched from floor to ceiling. The fire sizzled merrily, casting wavering shadows on the features of the lone figure in the room seated behind a mahogany desk, lost in contemplation. Despite the warmth, a chill settled in William Norrington's heart.

He stared out the window to the well-manicured garden beyond, his handsome face brooding. Black hair, artfully tousled, framed a round face sculpted by time and lineage. Ocean-blue eyes, usually sparkling with life, were now clouded with something akin to dread. He rubbed his clean-shaven jaw and wriggled his straight nose with distaste.

Twenty-five years of age, he was the Duke of Ravenswood by title, yet a prisoner of an agreement made when he was but a little boy. Betrothed at the age of nine to Lady Letitia Garvey, matrimony awaited him just as the clock ticked towards her debut season. He had honed his skills at dodging mothers and their daughters, who wanted a satisfying union in wedlock with him. Yet, his duty to Lady Letitia loomed larger with each passing day.

A sigh escaped his lips, ruffling the pages of the book he held but had not read. The door creaked open, shattering the contemplative silence. In swept his mother, Lady Elizabeth Norrington, the Dowager Duchess of Ravenswood. Her gown of pale lavender silk rustled softly with each step. She bore the regal air befitting the mother of a duke. Her blonde hair was bound stylishly in a chignon at her nape, her sky-blue eyes still held the youthful sparkle that had captivated dukes in their youth.

"There you are, brooding in the shadows like a lovesick poet," she chided, her voice as rich as velvet. "One would think you were about to face the gallows, not a courtesy call." Her beautiful oval face held a teasing smile.

William managed a wry smile. "The shadows seem more appealing than the prospect of tea with the Garveys, Mother."

"But you know Letitia's season is upon us, William."

He sighed, barely raising his eyes to acknowledge her presence. "Must we revisit this topic?"

"We must, my son," she replied with a steady gaze. "Lady Letitia is soon to make her debut, and it is time you fulfil your duty. The Duke of Alberton awaits your visit."

"I have successfully avoided the clutches of the matrimony for years. Must I succumb now?" His voice held a hint of frustration.

Her smile softened. "Your betrothed is a charming girl, William. Do not dismiss her so readily."

"Charming, yes," he conceded, "but... not for me. Not in the way a wife should be."

The dowager duchess sighed, settling into a chintz-covered armchair across from him, her expression sympathetic. "I understand, my dear. Your father and Duke Alberton were as close as brothers, two peas in a pod. They made this agreement with hearts overflowing with good intentions, wanting to bind our families closer."

The weight of those good intentions pressed down on William. He pictured his father, a jovial man with a booming laugh, and Duke Alberton, a man of quiet dignity, their friendship transcending years and ranks. He could not blame them for this well-meaning pact, yet the consequences felt like shackles on his soul.

"But times change, Mother," he ventured. "Lady Letitia deserves more than a reluctant husband, just as I deserve the freedom to choose my own path."

His mother's hand, adorned with a sapphire ring, reached out and patted his. "I know, William," she said, her voice softer now. "Believe me, I do. But Alberton has been through much since your father's passing. Letitia... she needs our support. A visit is the least you can do." She sighed and continued, "Both men envisioned a union that would solidify our families' ties. It is a commitment, a duty, not to be taken lightly. You cannot renege on it now."

With a resigned nod, he conceded, "I understand the obligations. But does duty have to feel like a noose tightening around my neck?"

She leaned forward, her eyes searching his. "You are the Duke of Ravenswood, and with that title comes responsibilities. Letitia is a suitable match. It is time to put aside youthful pursuits and embrace the role you were born to fulfil."

His gaze drifted to the crackling fireplace. "What about love? Should I sacrifice my heart on the altar of duty?"

"Duty and love need not be adversaries, my dear. Sometimes duty is the path to a deeper, more profound love than one could imagine."

A heavy silence settled between mother and son, broken only by the distant sounds of the household. Finally, William spoke, his voice edged with reluctance. "I shall pay a visit to the Duke of Alberton. But I make no promises, Mother. My heart may be bound by duty, but it yearns for freedom that marriage to Lady Letitia may deny."

She nodded with understanding. "Give Letitia a fair chance, William. You may find that the heart is a malleable thing, capable of surprising even its owner."

He knew she was right. Duty, even an unwelcome one, was not something he could easily shrug off. He was the Duke of Ravenswood, after all, bound by loyalty to his family and the Garveys. Perhaps he might find love as well, but he did not reckon he would. He only wished he could put off marrying her for a couple more years.

"Very well, Mother," he sighed, accepting his fate. "A visit it shall be. But do not expect me to walk Lady Letitia down the aisle any time soon."

She laughed softly, a dry, knowing sound. "I am aware of that. You dance to your own music, do you not? But just because the tempo changes does not mean you should not enjoy the dance, at least for a little while."

With a nod of farewell, she swept out of the study, leaving him alone with the shadows of his impending burden. He rose, brushing off imaginary dust from his tailored charcoal black coat, showing off his broad shoulders and his ivory waistcoat.

He would visit the duke's estate on the outskirts of London. He hoped to God that he would not find it as boring as he envisaged.

Chapter Two

The carriage rumbled along the rain-soaked road, the sound of hooves muffled by the steady patter of raindrops against the carriage roof. Inside, William nursed a headache that rivalled Duke Alberton's gout in its ferocity. The visit had been civil, the tea lukewarm, and Lady Letitia, though beautiful and pleasant, was as insipid as a suet pudding without the spice. He longed for the open air, the rush of freedom that riding his black stallion provided. However, he could not shake off the lingering atmosphere of duty that clung to him after his visit. The discussion of alliances and marriage had left him feeling like a man sentenced to a lifetime of societal obligations.

As the carriage rounded a bend, a peculiar sight came into view; a flash of scarlet peeking through the downpour. He spotted the mishap with a frown—a splintered carriage wheel and a damsel in distress. A lady, drenched and looking disheartened, stood beside the broken-down carriage, her bonnet askew and mud splattered across the hem of her yellow gown. Without hesitation, he instructed the coachman to stop. When the carriage halted, he thrust open the door like a knight summoned by a damsel's cry.

There, drenched and bewildered, stood a vision. Golden hair, framing a diamond-shaped face showcasing a button nose and rosy lips like a miniature portrait, peeked from the yellow bonnet. Her brown eyes, wide with alarm, sparkled even through the drizzle. Beside her, a stout maid held a parasol that was doing next to nothing in shielding her tall and slim mistress from the rain.

Unable to stop himself, William gawked at the beautiful lady as his stomach fluttered with something strange. His heart thundered against his chest as he observed the lady who was also gaping at him with an unreadable expression. He felt as if he could stare at her all day and never grow bored. Her lips parted, and his eyes lowered to their lush fullness. The loud clearing of his coachman's throat punctuated the highly-charged moment.

William hastily looked away as he struggled to put his flailing emotions at bay. This was highly unusual for him. Never in his life had he gawped at a lady so rudely before. With a small sigh, he stepped into the mud with uncharacteristic chivalry, his black boots soiling instantly. A navy blue cloak shielded him from the rain. "What calamity has befallen you on this miserable day, my lady?"

A smile, as quick and bright as a lightning flash, broke through the lady's worry, causing his heart to tighten at the beauty of it. "Thank you, my lord, for your timely intervention. It seems this infernal wheel has declared war on my journey. I fear I am stranded."

"Where is the driver?"

"He has gone to seek help, my lord. Alas, I fear that he might find none, not in this ghastly weather."

William surveyed the damage to the carriage wheel half-buried in the mud, his brows furrowed in concentration. A light-heartedness suddenly engulfed him. He let out a wry chuckle. "It appears the Fates have conspired against you, my lady. But do not despair, for I am at your service," he declared, a playful glint in his eyes. "This broken contraption is no match for a determined man."

"Your Grace, you will be drenched by the rain," his coachman chipped in as he drew abreast with a black umbrella.

"Oh." The lady's eyes widened and she hastily curtsied, her maid doing the same. "Pardon me, Your Grace."

William gritted his teeth inwardly with annoyance at his coachman. He had noted that she had not noticed the golden crest of the Duke of

Ravenswood emblazoned on the door of the carriage, and he had been fine with it. Formalities bored him, sometimes.

"It does not matter," he hastily said.

The lady watched him, her eyes reflecting a mixture of gratitude and curiosity.

"Your carriage shall ride once more, unencumbered by the whims of muddy roads, but not today," he announced, a mischievous glint in his ocean-blue eyes.

Disappointed reflected in the depths of her brown eyes.

"Where are you heading?"

"London."

"Then if you do not mind my humble carriage, perhaps you could ride with me. I am heading there myself."

She laughed with relief, a sound as melodious as a songbird's trill. "I am in your debt, Your Grace. How can I ever repay your kindness?"

His gaze lingered on her beautiful face, and he replied with a bow, "Your company on the remainder of this journey would be repayment enough."

Nodding at his coachman to carry the lady's trunk, William, with a flourish, ushered the lady and her maid into his carriage, his heart lighter than it had been all day. He paid a runner to warn the Lady's coachman so he wouldn't wait for her. The rain still fell, but the sun seemed to peek through the clouds, reflecting the sunshine that was the lady's smile.

"You call this humble, Your Grace?" she asked, eyeing the plush black leather seats with amusement.

He shrugged. "Humble by my standards."

She turned to smile at him. "If you say so."

"I do say so."

"Are you always the rescuer those in distress?" she teased, her eyes dancing with humour.

"Only when damsels like yourself demand it," he remarked, winking. "Besides, a broken wheel is a small price to pay for such charming company."

She laughed and his heart squeezed again. "And may I know the name of my knight in shining armour?"

He bowed slightly, grinning. "William Norrington, the Duke of Ravenswood at your service, my lady."

Her eyes enlarged like dinner plates. "You are Sophia's brother!"

He frowned at the mention of his youngest sister's name. "Yes. I am afraid you have me at a disadvantage since you know who I am and I do not know your identity."

"I am Lady Sarah Robinson," she replied, her blonde hair now slightly tousled by the rain, adding to her charm. "The late Earl of Beckley's sole daughter."

He raised an eyebrow in surprise. "Lady Sarah Robinson?" He had heard his sister mention her name in the past. "What twist of fate brings you to this muddy crossroads?"

"I have returned to London after many years in Paris," she explained, her brown eyes glinting with delight. "My mother, you see, married a charming Parisian nobleman after my father's demise. I have been living in the city of love, absorbing its essence."

The corners of William's lips twitched into a smile. "Paris, you say? I imagine the city has never been the same since."

"You flatter me, Your Grace," she answered with a playful glint. "But I assure you, Paris survived my presence quite admirably."

As they exchanged witty banter and playful remarks, William found himself enchanted by Lady Sarah's vivacity. She was unlike the average lady of the *ton*, and her unconventional upbringing in Paris had left an indelible mark on her demeanour.

"Tell me, Lady Sarah," he inquired, his tone laced with curiosity, "what brings you to London now? Surely you were not seeking a muddy encounter with a duke."

She laughed again, a sound that warmed the chilly carriage and his heart. "I have come to be your sister Sophia's companion for her first season. She is quite the delightful companion, I must say."

He stared at her with a jolt. His youngest sister had mentioned something about a companion arriving for her season, but he had not paid much attention to it, assuming his mother had paid someone to do it. "Sophia is fortunate to have you by her side. And I, it seems, am equally fortunate to have encountered you on this rainy day."

Her eyes held a warmth that kept him bound. "Believe me when I say I am the fortunate one here. I cannot begin to imagine spending hours there if you had not come along."

They continued to converse with the delightful ease of old friends instead of people who had just met. She occasionally threw in dry comments that had him roaring with laughter.

As the carriage continued its journey, the rain outside seemed to fade into the background, leaving only the delightful exchange of words and laughter between them. William could not help being drawn to the unconventional lady who spoke French fluently and laughed like wind chimes in a summer breeze. For the first time in a long time, he found himself looking forward to the season ahead; not with dread, but with a spark of anticipation in the form of a damsel with a broken wheel and a smile brighter than the London sun.

Chapter Three

The grand study at the Ravenswood Townhouse stood silent, save for the soft rustle of pages turning and the distant movement of servants around the house. William was lost in thoughts amid the towering shelves of leather-bound volumes that bore the weight of centuries of knowledge. Despite the pressing matters demanding his attention, his thoughts stubbornly clung to the vivacious Lady Sarah Robinson.

The events of the previous day had continued to linger in his mind like a persistent melody, and the image of Lady Sarah, with her lovely eyes, infectious laughter, and tales of Parisian escapades, refused to be dismissed.

He rose and paced the length of his library, the crackling fire reflecting the storm of confusion raging within him. Lady Sarah had burrowed beneath his skin with the tenacity of a burr on a woollen waistcoat. He could not shake thoughts of her from his mind.

Reason, however, was like a douse of icy water. Sarah, charming as she was, was the daughter of an Earl, hardly a perfect match for the Duke of Ravenswood. Letitia, on the other hand, was a Duke's daughter with a dowry that glittered like the crown jewels themselves. With her hefty dowry, he could increase his business pursuits to grow the family's fortune despite Charlotte, his immediate younger sister's husband's assistance thus far. Duty and prudence dictated his path, a straight line leading to the altar with Letitia, not exhilarating escapades with Sarah.

He sank into his leather armchair, a frustrated groan escaping his lips. Even a book, usually a haven, offered no solace today. The words blurred before his eyes, mere black scribbles incapable of taking away his turmoil.

A soft knock drew him from his reverie. "Come in."

The door creaked open to reveal Lady Sarah. Her eyes widened in surprise. "I did not know you were in." She hastily curtsied. "Good day, Your Grace," she greeted him with a smile, her blonde hair cascading in loose curls around her shoulders. "I trust I find you in good spirits."

"Indeed, Lady Sarah," William replied, setting the book aside. He rose, the floorboards sighing under his boots. "Come in. Please call me William."

She stepped inside, a vision in cerulean silk, leaving the door ajar for propriety's sake. Her presence filled the room with a breath of fresh air. "Thank you, Your Grace."

"William," he corrected.

She hesitated. "Is it proper? Given your station and mine?" she asked, her voice a velvet whisper.

"You will be living under my roof in the coming months. Let us dispel formalities. I find them burdensome."

She stared at him with scepticism.

He sighed. "If you are not comfortable with it, then you may only use my title when we are in public."

A smile curled the corners of her lips. "Very well then, William. You must call me Sarah as well."

"Of course." He strode forward. "And how may I be of service to you today?"

"I was hoping to borrow a book, with Sophia's permission, of course."

"What do you seek to read?"

"A book to transport me to distant lands, far beyond the confines of these walls," she explained, her eyes sparkling with a sense of adventure. "Perhaps some travelogue, something adventurous?"

He felt a thrill run through him. Adventurous indeed, much like

DAISY LANDISH

herself. He gestured towards the shelves. "The world of literature is at your disposal, my lady. I am sure we can find a volume that suits your tastes."

He led her to a shelf brimming with leather-bound volumes, their titles whispering of exotic lands and intrepid travellers.

As Sarah perused the titles, William studied her profile. There was an air of mystery about her, a captivating blend of sophistication and free-spiritedness that intrigued him. She was not the conventional debutante, content to flutter about in ballrooms. Her desire to explore the world mirrored his own yearning for freedom, and it both fascinated and troubled him.

"Tell me, Sarah," he began, leaning against the book-laden shelf, "what other corners of the world have you explored in your travels?" he inquired, trying to divert his mind from the riotous thoughts that swirled within.

Her eyes lit up with excitement. "Oh, I have been to America. The vibrancy of New Orleans is exhilarating."

"America," he murmured, picking out a worn book, "I hear the wild frontier beckons with untamed spirit."

"Yes, indeed," she responded with enthusiasm. "America is a land of vast landscapes and intriguing cultures. I also visited the bustling streets of New York and the wild wilderness of the West. It left an indelible mark on my adventurous spirit."

He raised an eyebrow. "The West? A lady of your age and station venturing into the untamed territories?"

She laughed, a sound that echoed through the library like a melodious symphony. "I have always had a penchant for defying expectations."

He nodded with a pent-up expression. "Where else?"

"The West Indies," she added, her eyes sparkling. "With emerald jungles and coral reefs bursting with colour."

He could not conceal his fascination. "America and the West Indies? Quite adventurous for a young lady."

"Adventurous, perhaps, but life is meant to be lived. There is a vast world out there waiting to be discovered. Fortunately, I have a mother and stepfather who share the same love for exploring."

As she spoke of her travels, William found himself captivated by her tales. It was as if each word painted a vivid picture, transporting him to the far-flung corners of the world. He could not help feeling a tug of envy; his life was confined to England and responsibilities while Sarah spoke of scaling mountains and traversing oceans. Despite her seventeen years, she spoke with the confidence of a seasoned explorer, her desire to travel palpable. He found himself wanting to join her on these journeys, to lose himself in the thrill of the unknown alongside her.

"And where will your dreams of exploration lead you next?" he inquired, his eyes lingering on the beautiful young lady who spoke of a world beyond the confines of society.

"Italy, perhaps, with its ancient ruins and sun-drenched vineyards," she mused, her fingers lightly tracing the spines of the books. "I long to wander through the art-laden streets of Florence and Venice. Australia also calls to me with its vast landscapes and indigenous cultures. It is a land of boundless mysteries yet to be unravelled. The Arab lands, with their rich history, are on my list as well," she breathed, her voice filled with awe, "with their Bedouin tents and starlit deserts."

A bemused smile tugged at William's lips. "Quite an ambitious list for a lady of seventeen."

She met his gaze, unwavering. "Age need not dictate the scope of one's dreams. Life is too short to be confined to the pages of a predictable narrative."

The truth of her words resonated with William, stirring a restlessness within him. Sarah, with her dreams as boundless as the horizon, seemed to embody the very freedom he yearned for.

"And what about marriage?" he could not help asking.

"I have no inclination to be tethered by the chains of matrimony," she declared, a mischievous glint in her eyes. "I aspire to be a woman of the world, free to explore, to learn, to experience."

He raised an eyebrow, feigning surprise. "Are you suggesting holy wedlock would impede upon your freedom?"

She laughed again. "Indeed. Marriage, for me, is an adventure of a different sort. I seek a different kind of companionship—with the world itself."

William could not help but admire her unconventional outlook.

"And what say you to those who argue that a lady's duty is to marry and secure the future of her family?"

"I say to them, to each their own. Some ladies look forward to such things, but I do not. My mother has an understanding of it, and she agrees with me."

Her eyes met his, a silent understanding passing between them. Their chance encounter, born of a broken wheel and a rainy afternoon, had sparked a connection as unexpected as it was thrilling. Duty tugged at him, whispering of Letitia and familial obligations. Sarah, with her tales of faraway lands and her burning spirit, had awakened a different kind of yearning within him. Once more, he questioned the well-worn path laid before him.

As she selected a book and bid him farewell, William could not shake the realisation that duty and desire were waging a silent battle within him. The daughter of an earl, with dreams that reached across continents, had become an unexpected muse, challenging the carefully laid plans that bound his future. And so, in the quiet confines of the library, he was torn between the allure of a world unexplored and the obligations that tethered him to the path of duty.

Chapter Four

The lavish ballroom shimmered with candlelight as William gracefully walked through the crowd at his friend's wife's birthday celebration. Dressed in a midnight-blue tailcoat adorned with silver embroidery, he cut a striking figure, his dark hair impeccably styled. The air was filled with the lively strains of a waltz, and laughter echoed through the grand hall.

His eyes, however, were on a different destination—the billiard room. Rumours just reaching him over Sarah's unconventional inclinations had piqued his interest, and he could not resist the pull to witness her defiance of societal norms. He had been surprised because he had not known she was also there at the party, and was even familiar with the host and his wife.

As he entered the billiard room, the clinking of glasses and the subdued murmur of conversation and cigar smoke enveloped him. Sarah, surrounded by a group of women who eyed her disapprovingly, sat at a card table, engaged in a spirited game with some men. Unperturbed by the raised eyebrows and hushed whispers, she played with a confidence that defied the conventions of the *ton*.

He leaned against the door frame, his gaze fixed on the scene unfolding before him. Sarah, with her golden curls tied with a chignon at her nape, seemed the epitome of grace as she played her cards. The corseted gowns of the other ladies seemed stifling in comparison to her flowing dress, a riot of colours that mirrored her spirited nature. An undeniable glow emanated from her.

Lady Featherstone, adorned in emerald satin that clashed spectacularly with Sarah's, harrumphed, "Playing cards with gentlemen, Lady Sarah? Surely that is unbecoming."

Sarah, eyes sparkling with mischief, barely glanced up from her hand. "Becoming, my dear Lady Featherstone, is a rather subjective notion, would you not say?" She dealt the cards with a flourish, the ivory rectangles flashing like lightning in her nimble fingers.

William felt a surge of admiration. Unfazed by the disapproving stares, Sarah embraced the unconventional with the grace of a gazelle traversing a jungle. He cleared his throat, announcing his presence like a ship arriving in a harbour.

Sarah looked up, her eyes meeting his with an unspoken challenge. The corners of her lips curled into a mischievous smile as she motioned for him to join the game.

"Your Grace," she greeted him with a playful twinkle in her eye, "care to try your luck against me?"

With a theatrical bow, he accepted the invitation. "I would be honoured, Lady Sarah, to engage in a battle of wits with such a formidable opponent."

A slow smile spread across her face, lighting up the room like a ray of sunshine. The disapproving chorus remained stubbornly silent, their lips drawn tighter than a miser's purse. He, however, relished the challenge. He settled into a velvet armchair, the worn leather sighing under his weight as he joined the card game.

The other women continued to glower, their disapproval solidifying like hardened wax. One, a wisp of a woman with rouge clinging precariously to her bony cheeks, sniffed audibly. "Some might say playing cards with men borders on...scandalous, would you not agree, Your Grace?"

He shot her a wry smile. "Scandal, dear lady, is often a matter of perspective. And from where I am, Lady Sarah's company is far more stimulating than any quadrille or insipid gossip."

His words dripped with defiance, a subtle rebellion against the suffocating norms. Sarah's hand flew to her mouth, barely stifling a giggle. Even the disapproving group seemed caught off guard, their whispers sputtering into silence.

As the cards were dealt and the game commenced, the atmosphere in the room shifted. The battle commenced, a war of wits and bluffs waged through diamonds, hearts, clubs, and spades. Sarah, a cunning strategist, moved with the precision of a fencer, while William, despite his best efforts, stumbled through the game like a lost puppy in a maze.

The other ladies, though reluctant, could not resist the magnetic pull of Sarah's infectious spirit. William played his cards with a practiced hand, yet with each round, he found himself more captivated by the lady across the table. The conversation flowed with an ease that defied the rigid limitations of society. Sarah regaled them with tales of her travels, her eyes sparkling with enthusiasm. The ladies, despite their initial reservations, could not help but be drawn into the course of her charisma.

As the game reached its climax, it became evident that Sarah held the winning hand. A ripple of surprise and admiration swept through the onlookers, and even the most stern-faced matrons could not conceal a begrudging nod of acknowledgment.

"Checkmate, Your Grace," Sarah declared, her eyes twinkling with playful triumph.

He chuckled, bowing his head in mock defeat. "I concede, Lady Sarah. Your finesse at the table matches your charm. Well-played." He offered her a gracious smile, laying down his cards.

She laughed, a sound that echoed with triumph. "It seems luck favours the bold, Your Grace."

Amidst the applause and murmurs of approval, Sarah rose from her seat, the picture of grace and defiance. William was captivated by her unyielding spirit. He knew, with a gnawing certainty, that indulging this burgeoning infatuation was foolhardy. Letitia's debut season loomed in his future.

The night continued with music, dancing, and lively conversation, yet William was preoccupied with thoughts of Sarah. He tried to convince himself that such musings were folly, that duty bound him to Letitia and her substantial dowry.

In the quiet moments between dances, he stole glances in Sarah's direction. She moved through the room with an effortless charm, turning heads and sparking curiosity. The more he tried to resist the magnetic pull, the stronger it became. As the night wore on, and the clock struck the early hours, he stood alone on the moonlit terrace, gazing out at the star-studded sky.

With a sigh, he tore his eyes away from the mesmerizing night sky. Obligation awaited him, a relentless reminder that refused to be ignored. Yet, as he re-joined the festivities, the memory of Sarah's rebellious spirit stayed with him. He could only hope that with time, he would come to enjoy Letitia's company as much as he did Sarah's.

Chapter Five

I wish I were somewhere else, William mused.

The grand Grosvenor ballroom shimmered in a sea of magnificent gowns and dashing tailcoats, a spectacle of lace and silk as the *ton* gathered for the first ball of the season. Chandeliers hung from the lofty ceiling, casting a warm glow over the polished dance floor. William stood at the entrance, resplendent in a black tailcoat adorned with burgundy embroidery.

The air vibrated with the thrumming of a string quartet against the backdrop of the melodic buzz of gossip and laughter. The dowager duchess, a radiant image in sapphire velvet, had insisted on this, the season's first grand ball. "Show your support and alliance, William," she had urged, her eyes pleading. "Let everyone see you and the future Duchess of Ravenswood in all her glory together."

She stood by his side, her eyes scanning the room in search of Letitia. "William, my dear, there she is," she whispered, nodding toward the beautiful, petite lady in lavender silk. "Go and ask her to dance."

William stared at Letitia as she stood amidst the crowd like a pale pearl nestled in a bed of fiery rubies. Her lovely gown, beautiful round face, and gleaming blonde hair could not disguise the blandness of her demeanour. His gaze drifted across the room, seeking solace in a different shade of dress and deportment. And there she was, Sarah, a vision in cerulean in the cloud of ecru silks, her presence as refreshing as a spring breeze in a stuffy drawing room. Sophia, his book-loving sister, clung to her arm, their enjoyment of each other's company blatant for all to see.

With a resigned sigh, William inclined his head. "Very well, Mother. Let us fulfil the expectations of the *ton*."

The music swelled, a waltz beckoning the couples onto the dance floor. All the eyes of the Garvey family turned towards William, anticipation heavy in the air. As Letitia's betrothed, etiquette demanded he dance with her first. But in that moment, something rebelled within him. Defiance sparked by Sarah's laughter, by the memory of her brown eyes and card games. With a bold, almost reckless gesture, he crossed the crowded dance floor, his gaze trained on Sarah as she moved through the throng of people with his sister.

The dowager duchess shot her son an admonishing look, a silent reminder of duty and decorum. Yet, as William approached the ladies, a daring notion took root in his mind.

"May I have this dance, Lady Sarah?"

The ballroom gasped, a collective breath held in surprise. Letitia's face paled, her hand frozen at her waist like a marble statue. The room buzzed with speculations as he defied etiquette by extending his hand to Lady Sarah for the first dance. The whispers spread like wildfire, the *ton* humming with scandalized gasps and incredulous murmurs.

"Surely, he jests!" exclaimed a matron, fanning herself in feigned shock.

"She must have bewitched him. I heard she is widely travelled. Who knows what she brought back with her?"

"Oh, poor Letitia!"

A hint of fire danced in Sarah's eyes, and her lips curved into a playful smile. "With pleasure, Your Grace," she said, her voice clear and bold.

They stepped onto the dance floor, the world around them fading into a hazy blur. Music and whispers swirled like mist, but all William felt was the warmth of Sarah's figure in his arms, the soft scent of lilac clinging to her like a secret. They moved in rhythm to the music, their chemistry palpable to onlookers. His hand rested confidently on her waist, and her gaze bore into his with something elusive.

As the dance unfolded, she voiced her displeasure. "Your Grace, this is highly irregular. The *ton* is scandalised by such a display."

He met her gaze with a smirk, a glint of mischief in his eyes. "Let them talk, Sarah. Just like you, I care not for the opinions of those who confine themselves to the rigid rules of society."

"A bold move," she murmured, her voice a teasing whisper. "I would not have put you down as a rebel."

He chuckled, a low rumble that vibrated through her hand. "Neither would I," he admitted, "but some waltzes demand a change in tempo."

The dance continued, a whirlwind of steps and stolen glances. The *ton*, still in a state of collective shock, watched as William defied convention with every twirl and dip. Letitia, left to the side-lines, wore a forced smile that barely masked her discomfiture. Her older brother, Lord Stanton, scowled from across the room, his fist clenched around a champagne flute. The whispers were now a hornet's nest, buzzing with conjecture and disapproval. Yet, William and Sarah danced on, lost in their own world. Her laughter chased away the discordant whispers. Her eyes, reflecting the candlelight, held a promise of adventures yet to be shared.

As the last notes of the dance faded, William escorted Sarah back to his sister's side. The dance had ended, but the tense atmosphere lingered. The room vented in hushed conversations, eyes still persistent on the scandalous pair. Letitia, face flushed with embarrassment, retreated to her mother's side. William's mother shook her head with disapproval. William, for the first time, felt a spark of hope, a glimmer that perhaps love could exist outside the cage of duty.

Before William could savour this newfound freedom, a liveried footman approached, delivering a summons from the host to his study. William excused himself with a bow, leaving Sarah amidst a sea of curious and disdainful glances.

A knot of apprehension tightened in William's stomach. He knew, with a sinking heart, that the price of his defiance would be swift and unforgiving. He would face the consequences of his audacious dance.

The Duke of Alberton beckoned him in, his face thunderous as he sat behind the gleaming mahogany desk beside The Duke of Grosvenor and his son. As William entered, a sombre expression etched on his face, the dimly lit study fell silent. A sense of foreboding settled over him.

Letitia's indignant brother's eyes bore into his with a challenge, and his voice dripped with disdain. "Explain yourself, Duke," Lord Stanton demanded, his tone biting. "What devilry possessed you to flaunt propriety in such a manner?"

William remained silent. What could he say? I do not want to marry your sister?

Lord Stanton's face contorted with fury. "Duke," he spat again, his voice laced with venom, "you have just publicly humiliated my sister and dishonoured her. Satisfaction will be demanded on the field at dawn!"

Chapter Six

The tension in the air hung like a heavy storm cloud as William ignored Lord Stanton after his declaration and faced Letitia's father. The prospect of a duel loomed, but William had no desire for such a confrontation.

"Your Grace," he began, his tone contrite, "I must express my deepest apologies for any offense my actions may have caused. I assure you, it was never my intention to bring dishonour upon your family."

The Duke of Alberton, a man of steely resolve, regarded him with a gaze that could melt iron. "Dishonour has indeed been cast upon my family this night, William. I demand satisfaction for my daughter's wounded reputation."

William sighed, running a hand through his dark hair. "I have no wish to engage in a duel with your son. Let us find a resolution that spares unnecessary bloodshed. I am prepared to make amends, whatever they may be."

"Make amends? The only amends you will make will be on the fields of honour," Lord Stanton interjected, his eyes still flashing anger.

William turned to him. "I offer my sincerest apologies to your entire family. My dance with Lady Sarah was not meant as an insult to Letitia, but rather a desire to break away from the rigid expectations of this season."

The older duke steepled his fingers, his face a mask of barely contained anger. "A desire, Ravenswood, in very poor taste," he rasped, "that caused untold humiliation to my daughter."

William winced. Shame for his impulsive actions washed over him. "You are right, sir. I acted without thought, driven by... foolish impulses." He paused, searching for the right words.

The older man stared at him.. "A bold sentiment," he finally muttered, "uncharacteristic of one destined for a life of duty and obligation."

"Let us get this over with," the Duke of Grosvenor interrupted. "Ravenswood has apologized. Do you accept it?"

A tense silence stretched amidst them, broken only by the festive noise coming from the ballroom. Finally, Duke Alberton sighed, a weary sound.

After a heavy pause, the duke relented, his expression softening. "Very well, William. Apologies duly accepted. However, the damage has been done, and you must take responsibility for your actions."

"Thank you, Your Grace. I shall get to it right away."

With a nod, William exited the study, a weight lifted from his shoulders. The ballroom awaited, a stage where he would have to face Letitia and, more importantly, confront the realisation that had struck him like a bolt of lightning.

Back in the ballroom, the festivities continued. The dance floor pulsed with energy as couples moved gracefully to the rhythm of the music. He sought out Letitia, determined to fulfil the expected duties of a future husband.

"Lady Letitia," he said, extending his hand, "may I have the pleasure of this dance?"

She accepted with a gracious smile, her lavender gown trailing behind her as they joined the dance. The *ton* observed with avid interest, eager to witness the resolution of the scandalous affair.

"My deepest apologies, Lady Letitia. I did not mean to humiliate you. I merely wished for a change in the order of things."

"It is fine, Your Grace. I understand."

"Thank you for your magnanimity in forgiving me so easily."

She offered him a brief smile and looked away, holding herself aloof.

Unlike his previous dance with Sarah which was filled with life, William felt as if he was in a cemetery.

As the dance progressed, William's eyes inevitably sought Sarah, who moved across the floor in the arms of another gentleman. Her laughter rang out like a bell, a melody that tugged at his heart.

A surge of unexpected jealousy gripped him. The realisation hit him like a thunderclap. Why would he be jealous of Lord Rushford dancing with Sarah? The absurdity of it all struck him as he danced with Letitia. He struggled for something to say to her to get his mind off Sarah, but he came up wanting.

A cold, hard truth slammed into him, undeniable and terrifying, a few seconds later. He was... in love with Sarah!

It cannot be! How is it even possible in just a few weeks?

But the truth stared him in the face. The adventurous spirit, the defiance in her eyes, the way she challenged everything he thought he knew about life; it had all conspired to weave a web that had ensnared his heart.

Panic tightened his throat. Love, unbidden and inconvenient, had reared its head at the worst possible time. He was betrothed, bound to another, while the woman who ignited his soul belonged to a different world, a world of freedom and far-flung adventures.

But hope could not erase the harsh reality. Chains of family, expectations, and a betrothal without his consent ensnared him. Sarah, with her independent spirit and wanderlust, could never be caged in the gilded confines of his life.

The dance ended, and Letitia curtsied with a demure smile. "Thank you for the dance, Your Grace."

William managed a polite response, his thoughts consumed by the vibrant Sarah, who continued to enjoy the revelry with other partners. He could not stand seeing her with men who were not prohibited to marry her, unlike him.

Unable to bear the conflict within him, William excused himself with a murmured apology to his mother and made his way to the exit. The ballroom, filled with laughter and the strains of music, felt suffocating. His heart thudded loudly in his chest as he strode through the corridors.

In the cool night air, he paused to catch his breath. The realisation of his love for Sarah, a lady he could not have, left him reeling. A mixture of emotions swirled within him — regret, frustration, and a profound sense of loss. With a heavy heart, he decided to act on the only truth that resonated within him. He could not go on pretending, bound by the restrictions of duty.

As the carriage wheels rolled across the cobblestones, William gazed out into the darkness, his mind filled with the image of Sarah's laughter, her recalcitrant spirit, and the undeniable truth that he could not deny any longer — he was in love with a woman who he could not be with. Despair clung to him.

Chapter Seven

Hours became days, each one a monotonous parade of propriety and polite smiles. William, his heart a leaden weight in his chest, clung to the flimsy hope that his love for Sarah would fade. He avoided the library, where the ghost of her whispered laughter lingered in the stacks. He ducked out of gatherings, dreading the mahogany gleam of her eyes that might pierce through the crowd.

The sun cast a warm glow over the sprawling Ravenswood townhouse, its golden rays filtering through the leaves of ancient trees. With a heavy heart, William had decided to distance himself from Sarah. The realisation of his love for her had struck him like a flash of lightning, and the only course of action, he believed, was to bury those feelings deep within and adhere to the path of duty.

Sophia, dressed in a riding habit of emerald green entered the study. Her eyes sparkled with anticipation as she approached his desk.

"Good morning, William!" she greeted him with a bright smile. "Care to join Sarah and me for a ride this fine day? The air is as fresh as a newly minted shilling, and Midnight just begs to stretch his legs."

He hesitated for a moment, his internal struggle evident, before he shook his head. He forced a smile, the effort stretching his lips. "Thank you, Sophia, but I have... urgent matters to attend to. Perhaps another time."

Her brow furrowed. "Urgent matters? But yesterday you promised we would explore the new bridle path by the lake! Please, William, come with us. You have not ridden with us in a while."

Shame, bitter and pungent, flooded him. He loved their rides, the wind whipping through his hair, the easy camaraderie with Sophia and Sarah. But now, every glance at Sarah, every shared laugh, felt like a betrayal of duty and a painful reminder of his impossible love.

He mumbled another excuse, a hollow echo of his fading resolve. "I am afraid I must decline, Sophia. Duty calls." He watched, heartbroken, as Sophia's disappointment morphed into concern.

Her frown deepened with worry. "William, is everything all right? You seem rather... distant of late."

With a forced smile, he assured her, "All is well, Sophia. Do not worry yourself. Enjoy your ride with Sarah."

As Sophia exited the study, William leaned back in his chair and sighed heavily. How he found himself in such a quagmire remained a mystery to him. He had never thought he would fall in love so suddenly. And the crux of the matter was that he was not in love with his betrothed, but someone completely unsuitable for him in the eyes of society.

Pushing away thoughts of his personal life, he focused on the business at hand. With the influx of funds and business ventures from his brother-in-law, he had stabilised the family's income after his late father squandered it in a secret life of debauchery. It was up to him to carry the family's legacy and not end up like the late duke. If he wished to do so, he would have to put aside his love for Sarah and focus on strengthening ties with the wealthy and influential Duke of Alberton, so his family would never again end up in the dregs they had initially found themselves.

After a series of meetings with potential business partners and his accountant, William sought solace in the solitude of the garden, where he stumbled upon Sarah snuggled under a willow tree, a book nestled in her lap. Sunlight dappled her face, turning her hair into spun gold and igniting a fierce flicker within him.

She is so beautiful. I love her so much. But...

His feet were rooted to the spot, a battle raging within him. He grudgingly admitted yet again that distancing himself from her would quell the tempest of emotions within him, that the cool facade of duty would act as a balm for the yearning in his heart.

The rustling of pages ceased as she looked up, her eyes meeting his with surprise. He quickly turned around and walked away.

"William?" her voice, like a forgotten melody, reached him. He paused, then continued his retreat, a coward seeking refuge in the shadows.

"William, wait!" she cried, leaping to her feet. He quickened his pace, the rustle of leaves masking the frantic drumbeat of his heart.

"William," she called out again, her voice carrying a hint of surprise. "Is something amiss?"

Ignoring her, he continued walking away, angry with himself for not being able to do anything about the path he found himself.

"William, wait!" she demanded, reaching out to touch his arm. "Why have you been avoiding me these past few days?" She caught up, her hand on his arm, stopping him in his tracks.

"Avoiding you?" He feigned ignorance as he spun around, his eyes cool and distant.

"Yes. What has happened?" Her voice was firm, her eyes a storm of questions. "You have been avoiding me like a rogue stallion spooked by explosives."

"Lady Sarah, there are matters that require my attention. I suggest you return to your book and allow me to proceed with my duties."

Her eyes narrowed with frustration and confusion. "Lady Sarah? This is not like you, William. We have always been able to talk openly. What has changed?"

His jaw clenched, and he spoke with a calculated detachment. "I have a duty to my family. My personal inclinations must take a back seat to the greater good."

She stared at him, disbelief etched on her features. "Your duty has never prevented us from conversing before. Why this sudden change?"

"There is no need for games, Lady Sarah," he spat, bitterness at his situation lacing his voice. "Remember your position, and mine."

Her eyes widened, the depths clouded with hurt. "Position? We were friends, William, confidantes who shared laughter and secrets over maps and card games. What difference does a season, a betrothal, make to that?"

His resolve, already shaky, crumbled at her words. "Duty," he whispered, the word a harsh rasp against his tongue. "Duty to my family, to Letitia..."

"A duty you never embraced with any warmth," she challenged, her voice rising a notch. "And Letitia? Do you love her?"

The truth, brutal and naked, stared him in the face. "No," he admitted, the word shattering the silence like a dropped crystal.

A flicker of hope, then of fear, danced in her eyes. "Then..." she began, her voice barely above a whisper, "then what does this change?"

But his courage, like a candle in a gale, sputtered and died. "Everything, Sarah," he whispered, his voice thick with guilt, "it changes everything." He pulled away from her touch, the chill of goodbye radiating from his hand. "I cannot... I will not... jeopardise my family, my name, for a forbidden dream."

His gaze bore into hers, his voice colder than the morning breeze. "Circumstances have changed between us. I suggest you respect the boundaries that responsibility imposes. Not everyone is as free as you."

Without waiting for a response, he turned his back to the fading fire in her eyes and walked away. Each step was a hammer blow, each breath a shard of regret slicing through him. He had chosen duty, yes, but the decision tasted like ashes in his mouth. He had condemned himself to an enclosure shackled by a love he could never claim.

Chapter Eight

The days that followed were an exercise in torture. Letitia, her pale smiles and insipid conversations about the weather, tea, and fabrics, felt like fingernails scraping a blackboard to William's ears. He endured her company with gritted teeth, feeling like a man drowning in molasses; every attempt to breathe met with suffocating sweetness. She was the epitome of decorum and propriety, yet her presence failed to captivate him. Each polite conversation left him yearning for the lively exchanges he once shared with Sarah.

His mother, oblivious to the emotional undercurrents, chirped about wedding finery and china patterns with the zeal of a magpie guarding a hoard of jewels.

"William, my dear, we must discuss the wedding plans. The date approaches, and preparations must be made," she declared, a glint of excitement in her eyes.

A sense of foreboding settled over him as he nodded in agreement. Wedding plans loomed on the horizon like a storm cloud, threatening to disrupt the fragile facade he had tried so hard to maintain. Each mention of the impending nuptials felt like a knock-back to William's already bruised heart. He wished now that in trying to escape from his love for Sarah, he had not told his mother that he would marry Letitia before the season ended.

With a heavy heart, he sought solace in the quiet corners of the house, away from the prying eyes and the weight of his burden. The realisation that he was to marry Letitia left him with a profound sense of unease. As he pondered more about it, he knew he could not do it. He could not marry Letitia, not when his heart belonged to Sarah.

"I have to talk to Sarah, to explain, to beg... something."

Driven by a desperate need for clarity, he sought her out in the library, their usual haven of whispered jokes and shared adventures. But the room, devoid of her presence, felt like a mausoleum. He found her in the garden, weeding a rose bush with gloved hands. She turned, her face a mask of cool indifference, the fire replaced by glacial frost. His heart missed a beat. He had seen anger, disappointment, and even defiance in her eyes, but this emotionless void was worse.

"Sarah," he rasped, the word a plea.

"Your Grace," she replied, her voice clipped, devoid of the warmth that used to melt his worries like winter snow. "Oh. It is back to being 'Sarah' again?"

He winced. "We need to discuss—"

She turned away, her voice cold. "There is nothing to discuss, Your Grace."

Undeterred, he pressed on. "I cannot bear this distance between us. I must know the truth. I love you, Sarah. Do...do you harbour feelings for me?"

A bitter smile played on her lips. "Feelings are irrelevant, William. You are bound by duty. There is no future for us."

He stumbled forward, desperation fuelling his steps. "Please, Sarah," he begged, "let me explain why I said all those things a week ago. You deserve to know why I..."

"Why you chose duty over love?" she finished, her voice laced with bitterness. "Did that require such a grand declaration, or could you have spared me the charade with a simple note scribbled on the back of a playing card?"

Shame, scalding and raw, washed over him. "I never wanted to hurt you, Sarah," he pleaded, his voice breaking. "Believe me, this... this tears me apart."

Her eyes softened momentarily, a flicker of the old Sarah battling with the icy wall she had constructed. "And what good, William, does your pain do me?" she whispered, her voice thick with unshed tears. "We are bound by chains. Love... it is a beautiful bird trapped in a cage."

He reached out, a desperate attempt to bridge the chasm that had opened between them. "Then let us fly away, Sarah! We can defy them all, escape this suffocating world, and... and..."

His voice trailed off, the enormity of his suggestion hitting him like a wave. Could he, in good conscience, abandon his responsibilities, hurt his family, and break their trust for a love that defied convention? He thought of his married younger sisters, Charlotte and Amelia, who had sacrificed their happiness for family duty. The memory felt like an icy hand gripping his heart.

Sarah, probably mistaking his silence for cowardice, pulled away. "It is no use, William," she said, her voice a resigned sigh. "We are a dream dancing on the edge of a storm. It is time to wake up before the music fades and reality bites."

His eyes, desperate and filled with longing, met hers. "No! I love you, Sarah. Damn the consequences. We could elope, start anew."

The mere suggestion hung in the air, a tempting proposition that could shatter the chains of duty. Yet, the weight of responsibility pressed heavily upon his shoulders.

Her gaze softened again, but resolve lingered in her voice. "As much as my heart yearns for such recklessness, I cannot be the cause of your family's ruin. Sophia told me about the sacrifices your sisters made. I will not be the one to bring about her unsuccessful season because of a scandal caused by us."

A heavy silence settled between them, the truth hanging in the air like unspoken promises. William, torn between love and duty, felt the walls closing in on him.

"We cannot be together. Please accept it as the truth," she whispered, great sorrow in her voice.

William, his heart breaking, knew she spoke the truth. He could not bear to see Sophia ensnared in the consequences of their love. With a resigned nod, he whispered, "Perhaps you are right."

He watched, his heart an anvil in his chest, as she walked away, her

DAISY LANDISH

golden tresses shimmering in the afternoon sun. Each step she took echoed the shattering of his hope, the fading of their forbidden dream.

In the days that followed, a sombre atmosphere draped over the house. Sarah, her decision made, announced her intent to return to Paris, leaving behind a trail of heartache.

That night, William penned a letter, confessing his love, his anguish, and his cowardice. He begged her to stay, to let him find a way to be with her. But when he presented the letter at breakfast, her face, though pale, was resolute in rejecting it.

"No, William," she said, her voice a whisper. "Paris awaits, and with it, a future far from unfulfilled promises. I refuse to live in the shadow of what could have been."

And so, with a final farewell and a shared glance that spoke volumes, she left. The carriage wheels crunching on the gravel were the death knell of his heart. As the carriage pulled away, he stood on the steps, watching the woman he loved vanish into the distance. Left with a hollow ache in his heart, he faced the imminent union with Letitia, knowing that the vibrant spirit of Sarah would forever linger in his mind.

Chapter Nine

William reclined in his chair in his study with no will to move on with life. Sarah was gone and with her, his heart. He had ached to go after her, but of what use would it be? She would still turn him down. And she was right. Until he got out of marrying Letitia, there was no hope for them.

"William," Sophia called softly, noting the distress etched on his features, his eyes betraying the turmoil within. "We need to talk."

He stared at her, weariness evident in his gaze. "Sophia, what is it?"

She took a deep breath, her eyes searching his. "You need to go after Sarah and beg her to come back. My season is not yet over, and I still need her."

His brow furrowed. "Sophia, it is not that simple. There are complications—."

Sophia, perceptive beyond her years, studied her brother. "William, you love her, do you not?"

His head shot up, surprise reflecting in his eyes. "You... you knew?"

"Only a blind bat would not," she replied, a wry smile playing on her lips. "All those stolen glances, whispered jokes, shared adventures, long talks, and hours spent in the study and garden with her. She almost bored me to tears talking about you." Her face scrunched into a frown.

"But why, brother? Why give her up? Surely love, even a forbidden one, is worth defying duty?"

He sighed, the weight of his emotions evident. "Sophia, love is a complex matter. Sometimes duty must prevail."

Her eyes softened with understanding. "You have always put duty first, but at what cost? Look at yourself, William. You are heartbroken, miserable by her departure."

He hesitated, then spoke with a heavy sigh. "Sophia, there are things you do not understand."

She crossed her arms, a determined twinkle in her eyes. "Then make me understand. Why would you let love slip away when it is right in front of you?"

His gaze narrowed, torn between the expectations of his family and the desires of his heart. "Duty to family and legacy binds me. Sacrifices have been made for the sake of our name."

She shook her head. "But what about your happiness? What about love?"

"Love is a dream, Sophia. I have to consider other matters apart from love. There would be a scandal if I were to break my betrothal to Letitia to marry Sarah. Your season will be affected. The entire family will be ostracized. I cannot do that to you, Mother, Charlotte, and Amelia."

She waved a hand in the air in disgust. "Please, William! Do I look as if I am dying to find a husband? The season has been a total bore, save for Sarah's presence. If I had my way, I would not marry anyone. I am rather content with my books."

He stared at her with surprise. He had always known that his youngest sister loved reading books, but he had not known the love transcended beyond being ensconced in matrimony.

Just as the weight of the conversation settled, a footman knocked on the open door and entered, bearing a sealed note. He approached William with a bow, presenting the missive.

"A note for you, Your Grace."

William accepted it with a nod, breaking the seal. As he read the contents, a range of emotions flickered across his face — surprise, disbelief, and ultimately, relief.

Dear William,

I hope this letter meets you well. I cannot tell you how sorry I am, but I cannot marry you. I have been in misery these past weeks because of the thought of marrying you. I do not know why our fathers thought it best to chain us to each other in betrothal when it is as obvious as the freckles on my face that we are not a perfect match. I have been in love with a baron since I was twelve. We love each other and have eloped. By the time you receive this letter, we will be on our way to Gretna Green to be wed. I release you from the betrothal. I found the contract and tore it before I left. I know you have itched to do so but for the sake of duty. I release you from your duty to fulfil your late father's wish. You are free to be with Lady Sarah, who I know you love.

Your former betrothed,
Letitia.
P.S.
My father secretly gave his blessings because he knew I was miserable. Only my mother and brother kept pushing me to marry you because of their fear of a scandal.

Joy filled him instantly. He had not needed to break their betrothal; she had done it for him. A wave of relief, almost giddiness, washed over him. He was free!

"What is it, William?" Sophia inquired, her eyes searching his.

He looked up, a smile playing on his lips. "Letitia has eloped with the man she loves to Gretna Green. She has released me from our betrothal. She said her father secretly gave her his blessings."

Her eyes widened. "Released you? But that means—"

He stood, the weight that had burdened him lifting. "It means that I am free to pursue the one I love."

"Go after her, William. Do not let her get too far," she urged.

He moved towards the door, his steps quickening with newfound purpose. Sophia followed, clapping her hands with glee.

As he hurried out of the study, the gravity of his decision bore down on him. Duty had been his constant companion, but love, it seemed, demanded its rightful place. In the grand foyer, he paused to gather his thoughts. The realization of the path ahead, one where duty and love could coexist, filled him with a sense of liberation.

Sophia, watching her brother, could not help but smile. "Follow your heart, William," she urged again. "The carriage is already waiting. I had wanted to go to the park to read."

With a grateful nod, a hug, and a kiss on her cheek, he set forth on a journey that defied the conventions of his upbringing. The prospect of love, once deemed incompatible with duty, now beckoned him with the promise of a future where his heart could finally find solace.

As the carriage rolled away, he could not help but marvel at the unexpected turn of events. Love, it seemed, had a way of surprising even the most steadfast hearts.

Chapter Ten

The rolling hills and winding roads stretched before William as his carriage sped toward the destination that held the key to his heart's desire. The pursuit of love had propelled him on, and the thrill of the chase coursed through his veins. He hoped he would find her before she reached Paris. Even if he did not, he was prepared to comb the entire city of love to find his beloved.

Arriving at the familiar crossroads, William's keen eyes scanned the surroundings, and there she was — Sarah, her carriage once again beset by a broken wheel. Just as fate had brought them together once before by a fortuitous carriage breakdown, his luck smiled on him again. Beside the askew carriage, bathed in the golden glow of the sun, stood Sarah, her lovely brown eyes wide with a mixture of surprise and... was that joy? Her maid stood beside her, gawking at him.

A wry smile tugged at his lips as he stepped out of his carriage, ready to offer his assistance.

"Lady Sarah, it appears that fate has a peculiar sense of humour," he remarked, a twinkle in his eye.

She looked up, her expression a delightful mixture of surprise and amusement. "Your Grace, is this a coincidence or some divine intervention?"

He laughed, the sound a joyous release after weeks of suffocating silence and sorrow. "Let us call it destiny's encore." He gestured toward the carriage. "It seems your carriage has a penchant for breaking wheels whenever we cross paths."

She joined in his laughter, the melodious sound echoing through the countryside. "Perhaps it is a sign that I am destined to remain stranded in your company." A playful smile curved on her lips. "It seems fate enjoys playing matchmaker. Broken carriages do seem to be your forte."

"I take it that the driver has gone to seek help," he asked, looking around as her maid walked away to give them some privacy.

"You guessed right."

He extended a hand, a playful glint in his eyes. "Allow me to be your gallant rescuer once more, my lady."

"Surely not. I am heading to Paris and you, sir, have obligations here in London," she responded in a cool tone.

He shook his head, grinning. "Not anymore."

Her forehead creased. "What are you talking about?"

"Sarah, there is a matter of great importance I wish to discuss."

She raised an eyebrow. "Oh, and what might that be, Your Grace?"

He took a deep breath, his gaze earnest. "Letitia has released me from our betrothal. I am free to follow my heart."

Her eyes widened. "Released? But why?"

He quickly explained Letitia's elopement, the release from the betrothal, and the exhilarating freedom that now pulsed through his veins. His words tumbled out, a torrent of joy and relief, his eyes never leaving her face.

She lowered her gaze for a moment and then lifted it, her expression guarded. "What does this mean?"

He hesitated, choosing his words carefully. "It means she has found love elsewhere, and I believe it is a blessing in disguise. It has given me the freedom to pursue the one I truly love."

A blend of emotions played across her features— surprise, disbelief, and finally, a slow bloom of warmth that reflected the sunset.

A moment of silence hung between them, charged with unspoken sentiments. She broke into a smile, a glimmer of hope in her eyes. "And who might that be, Your Grace?"

He stepped closer, his voice a gentle caress. "It is you, Lady Sarah Robinson. I love you. Will you grant me the privilege of courting you?"

Her eyes glistened with tears, and a genuine warmth radiated from her. "William, you need not ask permission. You have my consent."

Relief and joy flooded his heart, and he could not resist a playful quip. "I must say, my lady, this is a far more enjoyable encounter with a broken wheel than the last."

She laughed, the sound echoing in the crisp air. "Indeed, Your Grace. Perhaps fate has a way of steering us toward unexpected joys."

He drew abreast, brushing a strand of her hair back behind her ear.

"So, William," she said, her eyes twinkling, "shall we return to your townhouse?"

He held her gaze steadily. "Yes. For now. But after our wedding, we will go to Paris."

"Paris?"

"Yes. To dance with you across Parisian rooftops, to fill your days with laughter and your nights with whispers of love."

Her eyes gleamed with tears of joy.

"And from there to Italy, Australia, the Arab lands, and even to the ends of the earth."

"Oh, William!"

He took a step closer, his hand reaching for hers. "But only if you allow me," he added, a flicker of uncertainty shimmering in his eyes. "If you allow me to tour the map of life and bliss with you in holy matrimony."

She nodded with tears streaming down her face, bereft of words from the joy radiating in her eyes. At that moment, they sealed their pact with a kiss. It was a kiss born of longing, of defiance, of a love that had survived challenges.

Hand in hand, they walked to his carriage. As they resumed their journey, a newfound understanding and shared laughter marked the beginning of a courtship borne of tested love.

The End

Enlightening The Lady

CLEAN REGENCY ROMANCE

Chapter One

Lady Sophia Norrington gazed out the window of the drawing room in the Norrington Manor, her thoughts heavy with her looming second season in London a few weeks away. Her first season would have been a success as she had suitors vying for her hand, but she had not fancied any of them, much to her mother's displeasure. Alas, that meant she had another season to find the perfect match.

The sight of the vibrant gardens that surrounded the estate did not lift her mood and their colours dancing in the sunlight failed to bring a smile to her oval face like they were wont to do in the past.

Sarah, her dearest friend and confidante, was now married to Sophia's brother and lived away in Paris. The prospect of facing the social whirlwind alone was daunting.

She released a heavy sigh, gathering her resolve, and turned to look at her mother, Lady Elizabeth Norrington, the Dowager Duchess of Ravenswood. The older woman, despite having borne four children, was still a vision of regal elegance in a gown of sky-blue silk that complemented her eyes and blonde hair. The room radiated an air of refinement, with beautifully carved furniture and delicate artefacts.

"Sophia, you look troubled. You have hardly touched your tea and biscuits," she said, staring at her daughter with a worried frown on her oval face. "What ails you?"

Sophia hesitated, pulling back a loose strand of her black hair behind her ear, then decided to speak her mind. "Mother, I do not wish to partake in the upcoming season. With Sarah away, I find no joy in the prospect of attending soirees alone."

Her mother sighed, her expression softening with understanding. "My darling, I know it can be unnerving, but you must not let your heart be troubled. Forget about your first season. You will have a wonderful second season. Your sisters had immensely successful seasons. The expectations for you are also high."

Sophia's shoulders slumped under the weight of those expectations. "Must I follow in Charlotte and Amelia's footsteps? I wish for a quieter life, free from the confines of society."

Her mother regarded her with a mixture of sympathy and firmness. "You are a Norrington, and duty often requires sacrifices. A successful season would not only honour our family but also secure your future."

"But I do not wish to wed. I wish to be left alone with my books and sense of adventure. Must I be tied to a man to make my life seem worth living?" she questioned with displeasure.

"Oh, Sophia. If only you knew what loneliness awaits you without a husband, a companion in your later years," her mother said with a sadness that robbed her of words for a few minutes.

"Marriage is a beautiful thing, my dear, particularly if you marry someone you love. So, do not look at it like a terrible experience."

Sophia wanted to argue further but she knew it would be futile. She had listened to the same sermons during her first season. Feeling defeated, she nodded. "Very well, Mother. I shall embrace the coming season with pomp."

She frowned. "There is no need to be sarcastic, my dear."

Sophia sighed. "May I be excused?"

Her mother nodded. The burden of tradition weighed heavily on her, threatening to stifle the very essence of who she was as she walked out of the drawing room.

In an attempt to clear her mind, she sought solace in one of her favourite activities. She hurried to her bedchamber to change into a dark blue riding gear that displayed her slightly full figure before going to the stables to instruct a stable lad to saddle her favourite mare, Beauty. The extensive estate offered a sanctuary of greenery and tranquillity. As she rode along the winding paths with the wind tousling her black hair, she lifted her face to the warmth of the sun. Her mother would definitely frown at the fact she was without a hat to shield her from the sun's rays and avoid getting freckles. But she loved the sun and the outdoors. The regular clopping of her horse's hooves provided a comforting sound to her troubled heart.

Near a secluded stream, she dismounted and steered the horse down a narrow path that led to her private spot, a haven where she often escaped to. To her surprise, beneath the shade of an ancient oak, a figure was lounged against the gnarled trunk, a book propped open upon his lap.

Fury pulsed through Sophia's veins. This sacred haven, her refuge from societal strictures and familial pressures, had been violated. The audacity! Her anger, however, was overshadowed by a grudging appreciation for the intruder. He was undeniably handsome, his dark blonde hair catching the sunlight like spun gold, and his features carved with the precision of a Greek statue. His long legs stretched out lazily from beneath a coat of fine wool, a hint of emerald silk peeking from beneath the open waistcoat.

Sophia cleared her throat pointedly, but the man remained blissfully oblivious, his brow creased in concentration. Her anger returned and bubbled within her. This was her sanctuary, her escape, and she would not tolerate it being invaded. Taking a deep breath, she launched into a tirade.

"Excuse me, sir!" she exclaimed, her voice cutting through the serene atmosphere. "Do you have the slightest notion of etiquette? This is private property, and by trespassing, you have committed a most egregious error. I suggest you leave immediately."

The man looked up from his book, his dark brown eyes meeting her sky-blue ones with a calm that only increased her irritation. "My apologies," he drawled, his voice a velvety caress. "I seem to have stumbled upon this delightful spot without realising its significance. Pray, forgive my inadvertent transgression."

His charm, undeniable though it was, did little to soothe her ruffled feathers. "Significance?" she echoed, her tone tart. "This is my private refuge, not a public picnic ground!"

A faint smile curved his firm lips. "I see," he said, his gaze sweeping over her with an unnerving intensity. "And do you often grace this haven in riding attire, or is today a special occasion?"

Sophia bristled. "That is none of your concern, sir! Now, unless you have a burning desire to sample the wrath of a Norrington, I suggest you take your leave and never return."

The man chuckled, a low, rumbling sound that sent warmth spreading through her. "A spirited one, I see," he murmured. "Again, my apologies. I did not mean to intrude."

Her frustration grew. "Apologies are not enough. This is my place, and I demand that you vacate it at once."

He closed the book, a calm smile playing on his lips. "Your place, you say? I was not aware that the countryside had exclusive ownership."

Her eyes narrowed. "I have frequented this spot for years. It is my sanctuary, and I will not have it disrupted."

Undeterred, the man rose to his feet, folding the book under his arm. "Very well, Lady...?"

"Sophia," she replied curtly. "Lady Sophia Norrington."

He executed a slight bow. "Stephen Morton, at your service. I assure you, Lady Sophia, my intent was not to disturb your peace."

Sophia's anger simmered beneath the surface, but there was an unexpected spark in the man's eyes that intrigued her.

"Your service is not required, Mr Morton," she retorted. "Please, kindly leave."

Instead of complying, he leaned against the tree, a hint of amusement in his gaze. "I believe the countryside is vast enough for two souls seeking solace. Perhaps we can share this space."

She huffed, crossing her arms. "I am in no mood for company. Leave, or I shall have to summon someone to remove you from here."

He raised an eyebrow, his demeanour unshaken. "Ah, Lady Sophia, surely we can find a compromise. I shall remain as quiet as a mouse and not disturb your peace."

She grumbled inwardly, realising that convincing the determined man to leave would be an exercise in futility. And she could not stay either, for propriety frowned upon it. As she decided to retreat, she could not shake the feeling that this encounter would be the start of something unexpected.

Chapter Two

Sophia's hand hovered over Beauty's reins, her anger battling with a begrudging curiosity. This infuriatingly handsome stranger, with his cavalier disregard for her sanctuary and his nonchalant challenge to convention, had unexpectedly piqued her interest. He tilted his head, his dark eyes glinting with a mischievous spark. Sophia's lips, despite her best efforts, twitched with the urge to smile. Yet, propriety reared its priggish head again, reminding her of the unseemliness of a solitary lady conversing with an unknown gentleman. Sighing inwardly, she turned to leave, but the persistent man intercepted her retreat.

"Lady Sophia, I implore you to reconsider. The countryside is infinite, and surely two people can coexist in this tranquil haven."

She shot him a disapproving look. "Mr Morton, it is highly inappropriate for a gentleman and a lady who are not married to be alone together. Society frowns upon such indecorum. Surely, you must know that."

He scoffed, a playful glint in his eyes. "Society and its fastidious propriety matter little to me. I find the rigid constraints of the *ton* rather confining, do you not?"

She blinked, startled by his brazen disregard for the societal strictures that governed her life and the entirety England. This stranger, so unapologetically himself, was a breath of fresh air in the stale confines of her world.

"It is our duty to adhere to the standards set by society. It maintains order and respectability," she reminded him.

He chuckled. "Order, perhaps. Respectability, debatable. I have always found the *ton*'s obsession with appearances and empty etiquette rather amusing, do you not?"

A curious spark ignited in Sophia's eyes. "Perhaps not. Yet, the *ton* holds the purse strings of acceptance, does it not? Their whispers can sting like bees and their ostracism is a social death sentence."

He snorted, a sound that somehow managed to be both derisive and endearing. "Let them whisper then," he declared with defiance. "Let their tongues wag. Their approval is not needed and their whispers mere dust motes in the grand scheme of existence."

His words resonated with something deep within her, a yearning for freedom from the suffocating expectations heaped upon her. For the first time, the rigid rules of society and the endless succession of balls and soirees felt less like a necessity and more like a prison.

Intrigued by his unconventional perspective, she hesitated before relenting. "Very well. But I caution you to mind your words. We tread on dangerous ground."

He gave her a mockingly exaggerated bow. "Fear not, Lady Sophia. I shall be the epitome of discretion."

As they settled on the grass, a comfortable silence enveloped them. The stream whispered nearby, and the rustle of leaves accompanied the distant song of birds. Sophia surreptitiously studied the man, noting the neatness of his appearance despite the casual setting. His dark blonde hair, tousled by the breeze, added a certain rough charm to his refined countenance.

"So, what brings you to my abode today, seeing that you have never been here before?" she inquired, attempting to decipher the enigma before her.

He leaned back against the tree trunk, hands clasped behind his head. "A thirst for solitude from my friend's bustling house and the allure of a good book. What about you? Seeking refuge from the impending season, I presume?"

A genuine smile played on her lips. "You have a keen understanding of the *ton*. Yes, I find solace in these moments before society demands my presence."

He arched an eyebrow. "Demands, you say? I always thought society's summons were more akin to a royal decree."

She giggled, appreciating his wry sense of humour. "You may not be far from the truth. The *ton* has its expectations, and I have mine."

He surveyed her with genuine interest. "And what are Lady Sophia's expectations, if I may inquire?"

A mischievous gleam sparkled in her eyes. "To navigate the season with grace and avoid becoming entangled in the web of societal dramas."

He burst into laughter, the sound mingling with the natural melody of their surroundings. "An admirable goal, my lady. Although, I must say, avoiding societal dramas is similar to avoiding the rain in a thunderstorm."

She leaned in, her tone conspiratorial. "Perhaps, but one can always seek shelter and enjoy the spectacle from a safe distance."

Their banter continued, each remark carrying a subtle undercurrent of shared amusement. They dissected the absurdities of the *ton*, from the exaggerated manners of the elite to the complexities of matchmaking.

Their mutual disdain for societal constraints led them to a further spark of camaraderie between them. They further indulged in a spirited exchange of barbs, mocking the foibles and pretensions of the *ton* with acerbic wit. Sophia, surprised by her own boldness, basked in the liberating experience. They dissected the latest gossip, Sophia mimicking older ladies' nasal drawl when they disapproved of someone. He, in turn, regaled her with tales of daring exploits and unconventional pursuits, painting a picture of a life far removed from the drawing-room drudgery of the elite.

She found herself unexpectedly enjoying the man's company, his irreverence a breath of fresh air amidst the stifling expectations of society.

As the sun dipped lower in the sky, casting a warm glow over the landscape, Sophia realised she had lost track of time. Yet, the thought of returning to the stifling confines of the Norrington Manor and the approaching season filled her with dread. Reluctantly, she rose from her spot. "Mr Morton, as delightful as this reprieve has been, duty calls, and I must return home," she said, a pang of regret tugging at her heart.

He stood with a graceful fluidity, a smile curving his lips. "If we are not playing by the dictates of society, then please call me Stephen while I call you Sophia."

Her eyes enlarged but then she smiled and nodded.

He bowed with an exaggeration that made her laugh. "Until our next clandestine meeting, Sophia."

Sophia nodded again, a newfound lightness in her step. As she left the place, she could not deny the appeal of the unexpected companionship she had found by the stream. The elite might have its rigid rules, but in the quiet moments shared with Stephen, she discovered that breaking a few of them could be remarkably liberating. For the first time, she felt a flicker of rebellion ignite within her. One that she looked forward to intensifying.

Chapter Three

The next day, Stephen's unexpected intrusion lingered in Sophia's thoughts like an enchanting melody. His irreverent perspective and laughter by the stream became a delightful reverie she could not shake off. Eager for another encounter, she hatched a plan with a mischievous twinkle in her eyes. It would be a secret outing, a secret escape from the limitations of her impending season.

With the guise of calling on a friend in the village, she enlisted the help of the cook to prepare a discreet picnic. The kind woman procured a basket filled with delicacies. With her heart beating with anticipation, Sophia made her way to her favourite spot by the stream. Beauty, her trusted steed, acted as her accomplice. The sun cast a golden glow over the landscape, painting the scene with a warmth that mirrored the expectation in her heart.

As she approached the secluded spot, her eyes scanned the surroundings for any sign of Stephen. Disappointment threatened to cloud her expression when she realised he was not there.

He did not come.

Her shoulders slumped. Perhaps she was the only one who felt the connection between them the previous day. Or had she only imagined it simply because she had never been alone with a man before except her brother and male cousins? Mayhap she had been too hasty to think he found her company as entertaining as she found his.

What utter foolishness! I should know better than to behave like a henwit.

Just as she made to mount Beauty, the distant sound of hoofbeats reached her ears. She turned abruptly. A figure crested the rise, galloping on horseback, mane and coat billowing in the wind.

Stephen!

Her heart missed a beat. He dismounted with a breathless laugh, his hair dishevelled and cheeks flushed from what seemed to be a race against time to meet her. He looked as handsome as the previous day; even more handsome with his black clothing.

"Forgive my tardiness, Sophia," he said, his eyes alight with amusement. "My friend whom I am visiting in these parts required my attention for an urgent matter. It took longer than necessary." He patted his black stallion's moist head. "It seems my horse was as eager as I to reunite us."

His apology dissolved into a smile, warm and genuine, and Sophia forgot her disappointment in a wave of exhilaration. She smiled, her heart fluttering with excitement and relief. His unexpected arrival filled the clearing with sunshine, his presence as intoxicating as the scent of wildflowers.

"I am delighted to see you, Stephen. Your prompt arrival speaks volumes."

He gave her a bow and a radiant smile. "I aim to please, Sophia."

They settled on the grass, the carefully prepared picnic spread between them. The air was filled with the enticing aroma of freshly baked pastries and the sweet fragrance of blooming flowers.

"So, Stephen," Sophia began, her tone conspiratorial, "what literary treasures have you uncovered since our last meeting?"

He chuckled, reaching for a pastry. "You have a way of making even the most mundane discussions intriguing. I recently delved into a collection of philosophical essays. Quite riveting, I must say."

Her eyes sparkled with genuine interest. "Philosophy? An excellent choice. I find succour in the words of the great thinkers. Their musings provide a refuge from the trivialities of society."

Stephen nodded, a thoughtful expression crossing his face. "Indeed. There is a certain beauty in exploring the profound questions that transcend the superficialities of the *ton*."

As they delved into discussions about literature, their minds intertwined in the pleasure of intellectual discourse. Just like the previous day, conversation flowed with effortless ease, as natural as the gurgling of the stream beside them. They spoke of novels, debated the merits of various poets, and discussed their favourite authors. Sophia's voice was energetic as she described the witty social commentary hidden within Jane Austen's pages, while he entertained her with tales of adventure spun from the pages of Byron.

She marvelled at the ease with which he moved between topics, his intellect matching her own. There was an undeniable chemistry between them, a connection forged from their joint interests.

As the afternoon extended, their conversation shifted from books to more personal matters. They exchanged stories of childhood, dreams, and the aspirations that whispered in the quiet corners of their hearts. She found herself opening up to him in a way she had not with her sisters.

His laughter, a rich baritone, echoed through the trees, and she laughed with gusto with him, a sound she had not realised she had missed dearly. They argued playfully about the merits of heroes and villains, their voices rising and falling in lively debate.

The world around them faded, the sun reducing in its intensity as evening came. Sophia, lost in the captivating rhythm of their conversation, felt a sense of belonging she had never known before. Here, in this secret refuge, with Stephen by her side, she was not Lady Sophia Norrington, the marriageable commodity, but simply Sophia, a lady unafraid to laugh without caution, to speak openly, and to be free.

As the hours flew by, they lingered in the ephemeral bliss of their concealed world. The serene spot carried away the cares of society, leaving behind their intense connection and the promise of more stolen moments to come.

"The sun is setting," Sophia mentioned, barely hiding the disappointment in her voice.

Stephen gazed at her, the unspoken question hanging heavy in the air.

"Will you return tomorrow?" he asked quietly.

She could not tear her eyes away from his, their depths swirling with a promise of forbidden pleasures.

"Perhaps," she whispered, her lips curving into a playful smile. "But remember, good sir, whispers do travel. And I would hate to be the subject of some scandalous gossip."

"I must confess," he admitted with a genuine smile, "our conversation yesterday was the highlight of my day, and today has been more than exhilarating."

A warmth spread through Sophia's chest. "The sentiment is mutual. There is a certain magic in the moments away from the watchful eyes of society."

"Magic, indeed. I find myself looking forward to more of these clandestine meetings."

A spirited twinkle lit up her eyes. "Then, I propose continual defiance of societal dictates and revelling in the magic we create."

"So shall it be then."

With a laugh, light and carefree, she rose, gathering the remnants of their picnic. He followed, their shadows stretching long in the twilight. As they reached the edge of the clearing, he lingered, his hand brushing against hers in a fleeting touch that sent a spark tingling up her arm.

"Until next time, Sophia," he said, his voice a husky whisper.

And with that, he vanished into the gathering dusk, leaving her breathless and bewildered. The clearing seemed suddenly empty, the silence deafening. Yet, the warmth of his touch stayed with her, a secret promise burning on her skin.

The journey back to Norrington Manor was filled with a sweet taste of forbidden freedom that promised to reshape her world, one daring rendezvous at a time.

Chapter Four

"Oh, what have I done to myself?"

Sophia sat at her vanity, her reflection in the mirror reflecting the chaos within. Her heart resounded with the whispers of a profound emotion—love.

For the past two weeks, she and Stephen had shared stolen moments of laughter, intellectual discourse, and common interests. Riding through the outskirts of the estate, fishing by the serene stream, and losing themselves in the pages of treasured books, they had discovered kindred spirits in each other. She could not deny the warmth that blossomed in her chest when they were together, a warmth that went beyond friendship.

But how could she navigate these feelings that she could no longer contain? What did it mean for her to be in love with a man when the start of the season was a short time away?

"I wish you were here, Sarah, to tell me what to do," she muttered and turned away, pacing the room in her white cotton nightgown.

Her dearest friend would have told her what to do in such a situation. Perhaps if she spoke to her mother again about holding off on her attending the season, she could dwell more on her relationship with Stephen and see where it led.

With resolve, she made her way to her mother's bedchamber. She knocked briskly and was summoned in. The dowager duchess was seated at her writing desk, engrossed in correspondence. The scent of lavender permeated the air.

"Mother," she began, drawing abreast, her voice betraying the weight of her emotions, "would you spare me a few minutes?"

Her mother looked up, a warm smile gracing her features. "Of course, my dear. What troubles you?"

Sophia, twirling her hands with unease, took in a steadying breath and released it. "I wish to put off my second season. I am not ready to marry, and I believe a delay would be in my best interest."

A crease formed between her mother's brows. "Sophia, Society expects certain responsibilities from us, and you must fulfil them. A successful season will secure your future."

Sophia put both palms together in a desperate plea. "But, Mother, I do not wish to marry yet. I am just not ready."

Not that it has anything to do with a dashing man who I have fallen in love with.

Given her status as a duke's daughter, she was certain that her mother would frown at her developing feelings for a commoner.

Her mother sighed, her gaze softening. "My dear, I understand your reservations, but you must consider the greater picture. Your sisters have married well, and now it is your turn. Besides, the season is the perfect opportunity for you to find a suitable match. The older you become, the harder it will be for you to find a suitable husband. There is no need to put off the horrid day. Besides, I wish to see you married now so that I can have my greatest wish of travelling the world."

Sophia's shoulders slumped at the weight of her mother's expectations. "I know you have always wished to travel, and I know marrying me off will provide the means and time for you to do so. But, I—"

Her mother cut her off with a tender smile. "Sophia, my dreams have always revolved around the happiness of my children. If you find joy and fulfilment in marriage, then that is the greatest gift you can give me. But as you know, I always wanted a sojourn, but your father forbade it and I never had the means. With William's thriving business ventures, I believe I can finally have my wish granted."

Torn between familial duty and love for the man who was no longer a stranger to her, Sophia felt a wave of conflicting emotions. Her mother's sacrifices, her own desire for love, and the prospect of a life with Stephen entwined into a complexity that made her heart cringe.

Later, as she paced her bedchamber, despair clung to her. What could she do to salvage the situation and please both her mother and herself? Her sisters and brother had made sacrifices for the sake of the Norrington family. Was it her turn to do so?

Her thoughts drifted to Stephen, a man who, like her, sought a life unconstrained by society. She knew without a shadow of a doubt that she loved him with all her heart. Love, a force that exceeded duty, now pulsed through her veins. Yet, the knowledge that Stephen harboured a similar aversion to marriage brought a poignant ache to her heart. He, too, did not see the need to be thrust into marriage simply because society and family willed it. She had felt the same way, hence the reason she had botched her first season. But now that she was in love, she finally saw the beauty of holy matrimony. To be in a union with Stephen whom she shared many interests would be blissful.

She sank into a chair. The path before her diverged into two distinct roads—one leading to the pull of love and adventures, the other to the dutiful fulfilment of societal expectations.

Chapter Five

The following day dawned with a heavy burden on Sophia's heart. The air, usually filled with the promise of a new day, felt laden with the complexities of duty and love. As she wandered the estate, she tried to find a solution to her predicament, to no avail. She rode leisurely to her favourite spot by the stream, hoping Stephen's presence would dispel her melancholy.

When Stephen appeared, his usually cheerful countenance was replaced by a frown immediately after he gazed upon her face. Sophia could not conceal the sadness that clung to her like a shroud.

"Good day, Sophia," he greeted, his voice tinged with concern. "Is anything amiss?"

She sighed, her gaze on the distant fields. "Stephen, my predicament weighs heavily on me. My mother is adamant that I marry before the season's end so she can travel. Duty and desire to be free to do as I please clash within me, and I feel trapped."

Silence hung between them, the gravity of Sophia's words casting a shadow over the usual lovely and cheerful setting. Stephen's dark brown eyes, usually alight with mirth, now reflected a solemn understanding.

"I understand, Sophia," he finally spoke, his voice gentle. "Sometimes, the burdens of duty can obscure the path to one's desires."

Attempting to lighten the mood since he proffered no solution, she forced a smile. "Let us not dwell on sombre matters. We have another stolen moment before the encumbrance of the world descends upon us."

Stephen nodded with something akin to sadness in his eyes. "Indeed. What topic shall we indulge in today to escape the clutches of reality?"

Their conversation flowed, albeit with an undertone of melancholy. As they discussed books and basked in the simple joys of each other's company, she found consolation in the temporary reprieve from her troubles.

However, their sweet moment was shattered when the dowager duchess suddenly rode by, her expression one of stern disapproval and maternal concern. The horses' hooves echoed through the air, announcing her arrival.

"Sophia!" her voice rang out, cutting through the tranquillity.

Sophia and Stephen turned to face her as she halted her horse with disbelief showing on her face. Sophia immediately shot to her feet, blood draining from her face at the sight of her irate mother.

"What is the meaning of this?" she demanded, her eyes narrowing at the scene before her.

Sophia struggled to find words, her heart pounding with apprehension. "Mother, I can explain—"

She cut her off, her tone stern. "Explain? What possible explanation could there be for your furtive meetings with this man?" She glared at Stephen with censure. "I knew something was amiss when you came to me last night. How could you be so brazen to do this?"

Stephen stepped forward, a respectful bow accompanying his introduction. "Stephen Morton, at your service, Your Grace. Lady Sophia and I share a mutual appreciation for literature and the outdoors. Nothing untoward has transpired between us."

Her mother's gaze darted between them, scepticism written on her features. Ignoring Stephen, she turned to her daughter. "This is highly improper, Sophia. I will not tolerate such behaviour from you. Simply cavorting in the woods like a common milkmaid? Do you have so little regard for your reputation, for the honour of our family?"

Sophia attempted to reason, her voice calm. "Mother, nothing inappropriate has occurred. Mr Morton and I have merely enjoyed each other's company in joint interests."

Her mother's expression remained unyielding. "Mutual interests or not, such rendezvous are unbecoming of a young lady. You could be ruined if any of the village gossips sighted you. It would have ruined your season and caused a scandal. Mount your horse at once. We shall discuss this at home."

Stephen, ever the gentleman, sought to defuse the tension. "Your Grace, if I may—"

She silenced him with a stern glance. "No, you may not! Your interference is neither required nor appreciated, sir. You have done enough already as it is. Sophia, I repeat, mount your horse this instant."

Sophia cast a regretful glance at Stephen before complying with her mother's command. With a heavy heart, she mounted Beauty with trembling hands. Stephen watched them go, his expression a mask of unreadable emotions. As Sophia rode away, she cast one last glance over her shoulder, his solitary figure wrapped against the backdrop of the clearing, a silent sentinel to the dreams they had dared to dream. She feared she might never see him again. Her heart clenched with despair.

As they rode back to the manor in a strained silence, Sophia could not shake the feeling that the delicate balance between duty and love was slipping through her fingers, leaving her caught in the web of maternal dreams.

Back at Norrington Manor, the air bristled with tension. Her mother, cloaked in righteous fury, paced the drawing room like a caged tigress.

"How could you be so reckless, Sophia?" she lashed out, her voice laced with bitter disappointment. "Your conduct is beyond scandalous! A meeting in the woods? With a man of unknown origin? Do you have no sense of decorum, no thought for the gossip mongers who thrive on such impropriety?"

Sophia, eyes stinging with unshed tears, stood her ground. "Mama," she began, her voice firm, "it was not like that. We did not do any wrong. All we ever did was talk. We did not even hold hands, I swear it." She sighed heavily, a desperate plea in her moist sky-blue eyes. "Stephen...

er...Mr Morton—he... he understands me. He cares about more than titles and fortune."

Her mother scoffed, a humourless sound. "Understands you? A man who encourages secret meetings? Who throws caution to the wind? He is most likely a despoiler of innocents. A deceiver. My dear, you have been reading too many of your precious novels. This is the real world, governed by rules and consequences."

Sophia's shoulders slumped. It was glaringly obvious that her mother would never understand the beautiful friendship she shared with Stephen.

"Tis most fortunate that I found out before it became too late. Thank goodness I listened to my instincts and discreetly followed you. Who knows what would have happened? Mayhap he would have lured you into a false sense of security before taking advantage of you."

Sophia stamped her foot on the ground in protest. "Stephen is not like that, Mother."

"And how would you know? Known him all your life, have you?"

Sophia lowered her head as her eyes stung with tears.

"I forbid you to see him again. And do not dare to defy me." With that harsh command, her mother swept out of the room, leaving her in tears and despair.

Chapter Six

Two days later, Sophia, her spirit burdened by the clash with her mother, wandered the halls, seeking comfort in the familiar surroundings of Norrington Manor. She had thought long and hard about what her next course of action would be. At first, she had wanted to give into despair, but her fighting spirit would not let her. She refused to give up the one man who truly understood her. If it meant defying her mother and family, so be it. But then again, the thought of what her rebellion would cause kept her from wanting to do anything that would jeopardise her family's name and happiness.

As she swung her leg on the bench in the gazebo, the notion to salvage the situation suddenly took root within her like a fragile seedling. The more she dwelt on it, the more she believed it was the perfect solution to her predicament. With determination in her eyes, she concocted a plan to seek Stephen's counsel and to propose a solution that might appease both their desires and the expectations thrust upon them.

Shrouded in the secrecy of her resolve, she sneaked away from the manor under the guise of slumber to find Stephen in the secluded spot by the stream—the very place where her love for him had blossomed. The air hung heavy with the unspoken tension that lingered between them when they met again.

"Stephen," she began, her voice trembling with the weight of her proposal, "what if we were to break free from all the hindrances that hold us bound?"

Stephen raised an eyebrow, curiosity in his eyes. "Break free? What do you propose, Sophia?"

She took in a deep breath. "A marriage of convenience. We could maintain appearances for society while living our lives as we wish. A partnership that grants us the freedom to pursue our individual desires."

A pregnant pause hung between them, the birds singing and calling to each other above the only sound punctuating the silence. Stephen's expression remained inscrutable, his thoughts veiled behind a veneer of contemplation.

"You are aware," he finally spoke in a measured tone, "that I have no inclination towards marriage. It is a prospect that holds no appeal to me."

Sophia's heart sank, but she pressed on, her plea resonating in the quiet glade. "It will be a marriage in name only. Consider the alternative. A marriage that liberates us from societal restrictions, allowing us to live the way we want. We could be companions, sharing the burdens of duty while enjoying the freedom to explore our passions."

He remained silent and she carried on with anxiety. "Please think about it. We would live on our own terms. You, with your desire to travel and dreams of faraway lands, and I, with my yearning for adventure and a life beyond the confines of drawing rooms."

He shook his head, his gaze firm. "Sophia, I admire your courage, but marriage is not a path I am willing to tread, even for the sake of convenience."

Desperation clawed at her heart. "Stephen, please. I cannot bear the thought of a loveless union with a stranger forced upon me by duty. We could find a compromise, a way to navigate the expectations of society without sacrificing our individual happiness."

His eyes softened with sympathy, but his resolve remained unyielding. "Sophia, I cannot promise you a compromise that my heart cannot endorse. I am not willing to bind us both in a union just to please the *ton*. Even my father had to reluctantly accept that he would have to look to my siblings for his grandchildren."

"But... but we share so much," she stammered, tears blurring her vision. "The love of books, the thirst for adventure, and the longing for something more... more...and..."

Do I tell him I love him? Will it make him change his mind or will it make me look even more pitiful than I do right now?

Frantic now, she continued, "Do you not see, Stephen? This could be our escape, our chance to rewrite the script. There would be no need to attend multiple meaningless soirees just to find a bride and a long, winding courtship to satisfy society's stipulations. We could get married right away with the season beginning only a week from today. It would save both of us a lot of hassles."

He reached out, his hand hovering over hers before retracting with a sigh. "Sophia," he whispered, his voice thick with emotion, "you deserve a love story, not a mere bargain. You deserve a man who cherishes your dreams, not one who..." He drifted off and looked away.

His words, a bitter truth disguised as kindness, were the final blow. They pressed upon her like a crushing burden. She pleaded with her eyes, the vulnerability laid bare in her gaze, but his decision remained steadfast.

I love you, Stephen. Please do not do this to me.

"I did not wish to be wed, either, Stephen. But I am being forced to because I am a lady. You alone can save me from a fate that I consider worse than death."

"Forgive me, Sophia," he said, his tone regretful. "But I cannot be the answer to the dilemma that tugs at your heart."

Heartbroken, humiliated, and defeated, she turned away, her steps heavy as she retraced the path from what had once been a refuge. The stream mirrored the tears that welled in her sky-blue eyes.

As she emerged from the sheltered clearing, reality descended upon her shoulders. The marriage of convenience and the prospect of liberating herself from her mother's expectations had crumbled before her eyes. The conflict within her raged like a storm, and, with each step, she felt the tempest of emotion threatening to consume her.

Returning to the manor, she sought the comfort of her bedchamber. The tears she had fought so hard to suppress before Stephen now flowed freely, staining her cheeks with the bitter taste of unfulfilled longing. She allowed herself to grieve for the love that eluded her, for the dreams that lay shattered at her feet, and for the daunting reality that duty and love remained locked in an unyielding embrace, pulling her in opposite directions. But they were not what caused her heart to cringe with misery. It was the fact that Stephen did not love her. If he did, he would have gladly jumped at the chance of marrying her.

She held her face in her hands as her shoulders shook with sobs at the knowledge of unrequited love.

Chapter Seven

A week later, London embraced Sophia with its bustling streets and opulent townhouses, heralding the commencement of her second season. Days had blurred into a tedious succession of fittings and final etiquette lessons.

As she prepared for the first ball of the season, her bedchamber became a stage for the preparation. The swish of silk, the delicate scent of lavender, and the meticulous attention of her maid brought elegance around her. Sophia, attired in a gown of midnight blue with long puffed sleeves, a round neckline, and a full skirt with lace trimmings, felt the constriction of the night's expectations tighten with each delicate ribbon around her waist. Her heart felt like a leaden weight despite the jewels that graced her neck and the lovely gown that clung to her shapely figure.

The ballroom, aglow with a thousand candles, welcomed Sophia with a symphony of laughter and the rhythmic strains of a waltz. Admirers, captivated by her beauty, sought her company, offering compliments and filling her dance card. Yet, for Sophia, the accolades fell on deaf ears. Just like the previous season, prospective suitors flocked around her, drawn by her carriage and undeniable wit, but she was not impressed and found them all excessively boring. Haunted by the ghost of a love lost, she found every compliment insipid and every witty repartee hollow.

Her heart longed for the intelligent and lengthy conversations she had shared with Stephen. Alas, that would never be again. After the way he had rejected her proposal, she had stopped going to their favourite spot. With bated breath, she had waited, yearned for him to arrive at the manor and inform her that he had changed his heart and would gladly marry her. Even as the coach had driven away from the house for the journey to London with her mother, she had looked out of the window, hoping she would see him frantically riding towards them. It had been mere wishful thinking.

Arriving in London had been like a douse of icy water on her. Although her heart still longed for fulfilment, she had to do away with its yearnings and face the reality before her. She was destined to marry a stranger who would not share her interests, and she would spend the rest of her life in misery.

As she stood by the punch bowl, a fleeting illusion of escape, her gaze traversed the glittering assembly, searching for a respite from the monotony that pervaded the grandeur. She wished yet again that her mother had listened to her pleas not to attend the season.

Lord Westmore's butler's sonorous announcement echoed through the room. "His Lordship, Viscount Morton of Suxfield!"

Gasps and murmurs ricocheted through the crowd and heads swivelled towards the grand staircase. And there, bathed in the warm glow of chandeliers, stood Stephen. His dark eyes held amusement as he descended the stairs. The familiar lines of his angular face were masked by an air of nobility. The blue cravat, black coat, snowy white shirt, and trousers he had on were tailored to perfection. His black coat was decked with a viscount's coronet. She could hardly believe that this was the same man who had given her the impression that he was not titled now stood before society as a viscount.

Sophia felt the blood drain from her face as a wave of betrayal washed over her. The man, who had claimed indifference to titles and who had mocked the elite, stood before them now, draped in the very title he had denounced. The lie, clear as moonlight in a cloudless sky, stung deeper than any waspish gossip.

Anger smouldered beneath her composed facade. The revelation stung, a betrayal that reflected the hollowness of deception. The viscount she had shared sweet moments with in the quietude of Ravenswood had concealed his true identity.

Stephen, catching her eye, paused at the foot of the staircase. Their eyes met and held for moments on end, and it felt as if they were the only ones in the vast ballroom as time stood still. A flicker of uncertainty crossed his face and then it was quickly replaced by his distinctive nonchalant smile. He approached her, weaving through the throng of curious spectators.

Sophia held her breath as he closed the distance between them. He finally stood before her, looking as handsome as ever with a bow, a smile, and a hand outstretched, unaware of the storm that brewed within her.

"Lady Sophia, you look as beautiful as ever. Might I request the honour of a dance?"

The past, with its wounds unhealed, surged to the forefront of Sophia's mind. Remembering the pain he had inflicted when she asked for his help, she could not fathom granting him the indulgence of a dance.

Her response was curt and decisive. "No, my lord. I am engaged for the next dance. Even if I was not, I would rather dance with a donkey than you."

The shock on Stephen's face and the hushed gasps that rippled through the people around them brought an icy smile to Sophia's lips. She turned on her heel, leaving a wake of intrigue and speculation. The room, which moments ago had buzzed with the humdrum of polite banter, erupted in a flurry of whispers and curious glances.

The *ton*, avid collectors of scandal, hummed with speculation. Lady Sophia Norrington, renowned for her grace and intellect, had delivered a cut to the esteemed Viscount Morton of Suxfield. Gossips wagged their tongues, weaving narratives of pride, status, and perhaps hidden passions.

As Sophia sought refuge in the deserted conservatory, the whispers followed her like ghosts, spinning tales of a spurned debutante and a viscount who did not socialise much. Each murmur, each raised eyebrow, amplified her anger, a righteous fire against the man who had so effortlessly manipulated her heart.

Was this the man she had loved and mourned the loss of his company for days on end? The man who had spoken of rebellion and shared dreams of freedom from societal dictates? Or was he just a liar who played cruel games with unsuspecting, foolish, love-struck females like her?

The season, now infused with the tang of scandal, stretched before her. And she decided she would no longer be a pawn in Stephen's game; whatever it was.

"Sophia, do you desire to cause a scandal at all costs?" her mother suddenly appeared by her side and whispered fiercely in her ear.

"Mother, please, do not start."

Her mother gazed at her, sympathy clouding her anger. "Is that not the young man you were cavorting with back in Ravenswood?"

Sophia nodded, tight-lipped.

"When I asked you to stop seeing him, I did not mean for you to embarrass him in such a public manner."

Her eyes icy, Sophia replied, "Mother, it has nothing to do with what you said."

Her mother frowned with concern. "What did he do to you? Do not tell me you defied my orders and went back there and he—"

"It is nothing at all like that," she hastily cut in. "You were right. He is nothing but a lying cad who was merely playing games with my heart." She offered her a cold smile. "But do not be troubled, Mother. He has no hold over me anymore." Noting the keen, watchful eyes of everyone around them, she said, "Could we please go home now? I feel a headache coming on from all the noise."

Her mother looked as if she wanted to say something more, but then she nodded. She stared at her with concern before taking her hand and patting it.

The whispers might swirl, the gossip mongers might feast, but Sophia, with her head held high and a fire in her eyes, was ready to rewrite her own story, a story where love and truth, not deception, held sway.

The season had begun, and its most captivating tale was just unfolding. As she left the ballroom, the whispers of her words to Stephen reverberated through the crowd, leaving an indelible mark on her second season.

Chapter Eight

The following day dawned with a sense of anticipation, and the air felt heavy with the residual tension of the previous night's encounter. Sophia, driven by a tempest of conflicting emotions, sought refuge in the solace of her favourite park—the haven where the crunch of leaves and the whispers of nature were her companions.

Attired in a simple gown of pale yellow, Sophia, accompanied by her faithful maid, ventured into the embrace of nature. The vast park, a picture of greenery and blossoms, offered respite from the prying eyes of society. As she settled beneath the shade of a majestic oak, the pages of a cherished novel unfurled before her. The gentle swirl of leaves played a melodic accompaniment to the words that transported her to distant realms. Amidst the serenity, the wounds inflicted by Stephen's deceit pervaded her peace of mind.

How could he have shown his face at the ball last night after what he did? Was it to mock her? To gloat that he could actually marry her but he chose not to? If only she could get her heart to stop clenching at the thought of him. After spending a night tossing and turning, she was displeased that he still filled her thoughts.

"Is that book as interesting as Jane Austen's?"

The breath ceased in her chest at the sound of the voice she would recognise even in her dreams.

"Stephen," she uttered as she lifted her head to see him standing a few feet from her, her tone a measured blend of caution and curiosity.

What was he doing here? How did he know she would be there? Had he gone to the house and her mother told him she was there?

He approached with an earnestness that bespoke remorse, reading the questions in her eyes. "Sophia, I knew you would come here because it is one of my favourite spots. And as we share so much in common, I—"

"You do not have leave to use my name, sir!" she cut in.

He winced. "Please let me explain."

Sophia cut him off again with a wave of her hand, a gesture that demanded silence. "Save your words, Viscount. I have little patience for explanations."

The silence hung between them, the tension palpable. Stephen, with guilt marked on his countenance, sought to breach the fortress of her defences once more.

"I did not mean to deceive you," he finally spoke, his words filled with sincerity. "I came to London because of you. I cannot recall the last time I attended a ball, but I was ready to do anything to win you back."

She shook her head. She did not wish to listen to his lies anymore. She wished she could stand up and leave but her heart would not let her. With chagrin, she discovered they were gathering attention.

"Please leave, Viscount. I do not wish to be the topic of further gossip and speculation."

To her surprise, he chuckled. She lifted her eyes to meet the amusement in his.

"Does this in any way seem funny to you?" she snapped.

He shrugged. "Only that it reminds me of the first time we met. The only differences, I believe, are the location and who is seated reading."

She bit her lip and kept silent.

His smile widened. "I remember lifting my head and dragging in a silent breath, for I felt as if I was being visited by an angel."

She snorted. "Fine words will get you nowhere."

"Please, Sophia. I speak the truth. I found you incredibly beautiful and feisty. I did not wish to chase you away with my adoration, so I forced myself to maintain a cool façade while my heart beat thunderously against my chest. I remember going back to George and he knew instinctively that something happened to me. I told him all about you and how much I looked forward to seeing you again."

Sophia's chest tightened. She too had longed to share the news of meeting him with someone.

"Every morning, I woke up with a smile, knowing I would see you and spend some time with you. Every night, I slept with a grin, recalling the beautiful moments spent with you. I could barely think of anything else but you."

Then why did you reject me? Why did you let me go? Her heart cried.

As if reading her mind, he said, "It took not seeing you for me to realise what I felt for you was love. I fell in love with you but still held on strongly to my beliefs like a stubborn fool." He lowered his head in self-disgust. "After meeting you, my perspective on marriage changed." He lifted his head. "Sophia, my beauty, I love you. I am ready to embrace the commitment I once spurned."

Sophia's eyes widened with disbelief and something akin to hope. Could she believe him or was he playing another game? She desperately wanted to believe him but she feared for her heart.

Her lips pressed into a thin line. "Your charade ends here, Lord Suxfield. The man I knew would not hide behind titles, would not play games with my heart."

His shoulders slumped, his eyes filled with a profound sadness. "Sophia, listen to me," he pleaded, approaching her with outstretched hands. "I understand your anger and your disbelief. But the title... it was not a lie. It is a burden I inherited, not a mask I donned. I did not see it as important and I have never seen it as something I should be wholly proud of and announce everywhere I go."

His words, though offered with sincerity, did little to quell the storm within her. "Lies beget lies," she retorted, her voice trembling with indignation. "And yours, Viscount, were woven with such exquisite thread that a fool would not have seen through them."

He drew closer, imploring her to believe him with her eyes. "No, Sophia. I was the fool to have rejected the offer I desperately craved in my heart but instead foolishly used my intellect to reply to you." His voice dropped to a husky whisper. "My dearest Sophia, you have become the only reason I wish to continue living, the only reason I wish to be married and have children if you will be my wife and the mother of my children."

His words, uttered with a raw earnestness that cut through her anger, left Sophia breathless. Could it be true? Could the man who deceived her also be the man who loves her?

"I am a viscount, yes, but a viscount desperate to claim the heart of the woman he loves."

To her amazement, he went down on a bended knee. "Our meeting started tumultuously but eventually we became friends and I fell in love with you before making a terrible mistake which I am ready to rectify now and for the rest of my life if you will have me, Lady Sophia Norrington."

Before she could process the confession and accept his proposal, a footman, clad in livery, approached with a message from her mother.

"Forgive the intrusion, Lady Sophia," the footman spoke with a respectful bow. "But the Dowager Duchess insists on your immediate return. A suitor awaits your presence."

The news struck Sophia like a bolt of lightning. A suitor!

Chapter Nine

Alarmed by the urgency in the footman's message, Sophia turned to Stephen with a frown. "A suitor? I cannot believe that Mother is entertaining a suitor on my behalf."

Stephen spoke in earnest. "Do not let the message trouble you, Sophia. We shall face whatever awaits together."

"We?" she questioned.

"That is if you will have me."

She longed to tell him yes and how much she loved him, but the message from her mother had ruined the moment for her...for them.

"Please rise, Stephen. I will give you an answer after attending to my mother. I must go now."

"I will come with you," he announced, standing.

She frowned. "Why? Do you think that it is wise? I do not think my mother will be pleased to see you with me."

He grinned. "Fret not, my love. All will be well."

Summoning her maid a short distance away, Sophia hurried to the waiting carriage where Stephen helped her to climb in. Despite his words, her heart fluttered with apprehension as they made their way back to the Ravenswood London townhouse. The journey, though short, seemed interminable. If her mother had accepted a suitor on her behalf, she would be deeply cross with her.

Upon arrival, the air hummed with an undercurrent of anticipation. Sophia, her steps resounding through the marble-floored foyer, braced herself for the encounter that awaited. The butler informed them that her mother awaited her in the drawing room.

As Sophia entered, she found the dowager duchess in conversation with a distinguished gentleman—a man of undeniable refinement, his features marked by the passage of years. When he turned to look at her, and she gazed upon his dark blonde hair, angular face, and dark brown eyes, her heart missed a beat at how familiar he appeared.

He is Stephen's father!

Her eyes widened with astonishment and disbelief as she turned to look at Stephen.

"Why is your father here?" she questioned, her voice betraying a hint of trepidation.

Stephen, standing by her side, offered a reassuring smile, a silent affirmation of the unspoken conversation that had transpired between them.

Her mother, her gaze penetrating, gestured for Sophia to take a seat. "Sophia, my dear, I present to you the Earl of Wingate, father to the viscount you have grown quite acquainted with, I presume."

The earl, a man of dignified composure, addressed Sophia with a polite bow. "Lady Sophia, I have come on behalf of my son, Stephen. It seems he found himself entangled in a situation that required my intervention."

Sophia's mind whirred with confusion, the puzzle pieces scattered about. Stephen spoke, his voice a gentle reassurance. "I sought my father's assistance, fearing I had erred in our interactions and wishing to make amends in the proper manner. Sophia, I love you deeply, and I want to do right by you."

The revelation and clarity in the midst of uncertainty washed over Sophia. Stephen, fearing he had lost her trust, had orchestrated this elaborate play to win her hand not through deception, but through propriety.

A surge of warmth spread in her chest, melting the ice of anger and hurt. The man who had lied to her was also the man who, in his own clumsy way, was putting his heart on a silver platter.

"Stephen," she whispered, her voice trembling with emotion, "you did not have to."

He silenced her with a gentle finger to her lips. "Hush, my love," he murmured, his eyes reflecting the turmoil within him. "Let me face this. My father, your mother... let me prove to them that my intentions are true, my love genuine."

The earl, his eyes warm with paternal affection, continued, "My son has expressed his intentions to court you properly and, if you find favour in his suit, to request your hand in marriage."

A ripple of emotions surged through Sophia—joy, relief, and a newfound understanding. The earl's words, spoken with sincerity, resonated with the promise of redemption.

Stephen, with worry in his eyes, sought her response. "Sophia, I did not wish to jeopardise your reputation or cause you distress by not telling you about my title, and rejecting your proposal. Will you allow me the opportunity to court you openly, to prove the sincerity of my intentions?"

Sophia, her heart swelling with emotions, nodded in agreement. "Yes, Lord Suxfield. I believe in second chances, and I am willing to see where this path may lead because I love you."

A silence followed, the only sound the crackling fire in the hearth. Then, a tear glistened in Sophia's eye, followed by another. A smile, hesitant at first, then radiant, spread on Stephen's face.

"Sophia," he breathed with thick emotion, "you, my dearest, have read my heart better than I ever could. I love you. With every fibre of my being, I love you."

"Stephen and Sophia," the dowager duchess rasped suddenly, her eyes glistening with tears, "if your hearts are truly one, then who am I to deny your happiness? I give my blessing, and I feel blessed that I have witnessed love in its purest form."

"I give my blessings to. Love each other for the rest of your days. You make a perfect couple," Stephen's father concurred with a radiant smile.

Tears of joy rolled down Sophia's cheeks as Stephen cupped her face in his hands and sealed their agreement with a tender kiss.

Sophia embraced the prospect of a courtship that transcended the shadows of secrecy, allowing the tender buds of affection to bloom under the gaze of society's watchful eyes.

Chapter Ten

Flowers in every shade imaginable, spilled from overflowing baskets, their sweet scent mingling with the joyous thrum of music wafting from the open windows. The sun bathed the gardens in a radiant light, transforming the rolling lawns and fragrant blossoms into the idyllic setting for a fairytale wedding.

Sophia, glowing in a simple white silk gown adorned with delicate pearls and lace, stood beside Stephen under a canopy of roses. His dark brown eyes held a love that rivalled the spring sun's warmth. They had both desired a wedding setting that would bring back memories of how they met and fell in love.

A soft breeze carried the sweet-smelling whispers of flourishing flowers as guests in regal attire gathered in the meticulously manicured gardens. The colour palette of pastel hues painted the scene with an air of enchantment.

The garden, transformed into a haven of floral splendour, bore witness to the union of two hearts entwined by fate. Under the arbour decorated with white roses and ivy, Sophia and Stephen exchanged vows, their promises resonating amidst the delicate petals that swayed in rhythmic harmony.

As they sealed their commitment with a tender kiss, applause erupted from the assembled guests, their joyous cheers mingling with the melodies of nature.

Following the ceremony, the celebration continued in the garden, where tables with silver candelabras and crystal vases hosted an array of delectable delights. The guests basked in the festivities, their laughter and merriment reverberating beneath the blue sky.

Later in the afternoon, the newly-married couple stole away for a quiet respite. Hand in hand, they ventured into the heart of the garden, a sanctuary that mirrored the burgeoning beauty of their love and where they first met.

The garden path, lined with roses, led them to a secluded alcove with a wrought-iron bench. There, amidst nature's embrace, they found a moment of quietude.

Sophia, her eyes reflecting the depth of her emotions, turned to Stephen. "From clandestine meetings to London to this beautiful day, I am grateful for the journey we have shared."

Stephen, his gaze tender, spoke from the heart. "My love, you have brought light to the gardens of my heart, transforming them into a sanctuary of joy and beauty. Today, as we embark on this journey together, I am filled with gratitude for the love we have discovered."

She sighed with contentment. "I am still amazed that we are man and wife. When I rode to the stream that day, my heart in turmoil of the forthcoming season, I never knew it would turn my life around."

Her husband chuckled. "And I will forever be grateful to George for inviting me over for a visit. You see, I had quarrelled with my father over the marriage issue and George's invitation was a welcome respite from the tension back home."

She tilted her head to the side to stare at him. "Tell me, my love, why did you not want to get married?"

He shrugged. "I found it frivolous. An utter charade. I had witnessed many marriages from relatives that were mere formalities, in name only, probably to seal family ties, increase the family wealth and coffers, or just for procreation. I did not wish to be caught in such a travesty."

She nodded with understanding. "That was why you rejected my proposal for a marriage of convenience, is it not?"

He sighed. "I did not tell that day by the stream because I wanted to spare you trying to convince me that our marriage would not be like theirs. I believed in love, but I thought myself too cynical to find one who would love me just as I was; a lover of books, new things, adventures with utter disdain for societal dictates." He smiled and cupped her chin. "But I am eternally grateful that fate took pity on me and brought you into my life, my soulmate."

She beamed at him. "I am grateful too for the twist life gave me in you, for I had feared I would surely end up being married to a pot-bellied, much older man who did not own a single book to his name and would never understand my love for them."

He threw back his head and laughter rumbled from his throat. Love for him filled her as she watched him engulfed in hilarity.

"I look forward to introducing you to Sarah. She will definitely approve of you," she said with a glimmer in her eyes. They would head for Paris the following day on their honeymoon and be reunited with her best friend and her brother.

"It is a shame she and your brother could not make it to our wedding."

She laughed. "That is because someone was so eager to get married, he did not wait for the invitations to be sent."

He grinned. "I did not fancy a huge wedding. All I desired was for us to be joined as husband and wife posthaste so we could start living our dreams."

"As did I."

They sat in companionable silence for a moment, the swish of leaves and the distant strains of music mingling with their blatant love for each other. The promise of a future together unfolded like the petals of a rose, delicate and filled with the fragrance of endless possibilities.

Sophia felt so much joy in her heart that she feared she would burst with it. She had not only found a man with a like mind and mutual interests, she was married to him as well. Her mother could travel and live her dreams now that her four children were successfully married.

Stephen, his eyes reflecting the sincerity of his devotion, took Sophia's hands in his. "Sophia, my heart belongs to you, now and always. With each step we take, let our love be the guiding force that illuminates our path."

"And my heart belongs to you, too, my darling viscount, forever. I look forward to traversing the world with you and discovering new things. Only with you."

The End

Reclaiming The Lady
CLEAN REGENCY ROMANCE

Chapter One

The setting sun cast a warm, golden radiance across the autumn landscape as Dowager Duchess of Ravenswood Elizabeth Norrington's carriage rumbled along the familiar road to her dower house in Brampton. The crisp autumn air was tinged with the earthy fragrance of fallen leaves, and the distant chirping of crickets heralded the onset of dusk.

"Although I do not care much for the hustle and bustle of the city, I must confess that I shall miss London dearly," Elizabeth told her long-time companion and confidante, her maid, Susan.

The Season, with its endless whirl of drawing rooms and balls, lay behind Elizabeth, leaving a hollowness in her heart. Her four children had found love and happiness with their spouses, leaving her adrift in a sea of memories.

"It is good to be back home, Duchess," Susan replied fondly with a bright smile.

Elizabeth sighed. "It is indeed." Although she had not spent much extended time in her dower house after her husband's passing before going over to the Ravenswood Estate to supervise her daughters' seasons, she was glad she had a place to call her own. In a few months, she would depart for the colonies to start her sojourn around continents. She had postponed her journey until the following year because of her children and because she had been unwell after her last daughter's wedding.

The carriage slowed down, and Elizabeth peered out, her blue eyes the colour of the sky, catching sight of another carriage by the roadside. Her stomach clenched at the view of the lone carriage, overturned, laying in the ditch. As her coachman skilfully navigated the vehicle closer, a chilling realisation gripped her heart—a man, a victim of treacherous highwaymen, no doubt, lay sprawled by the roadside, his form obscured by the encroaching shadows.

"Stop the carriage!" Elizabeth's command sliced through the air, and the coachman brought the horses to a gentle halt.

"My lady, what is it?" Susan questioned with worry, but Elizabeth did not reply to her.

With the urgency born of empathy, she pushed open the door, lifted the hem of her peach dress, and stepped out onto the dimming landscape. Her eyes widened at the sight of the wounded man; his clothes stained with the evidence of a struggle. He moaned weakly, and her oval face scrunched into a frown. Compassion overshadowed any sense of propriety as she approached, her footsteps rustling through the fallen leaves.

"Help me!" she called out.

Her loyal coachman, Wilton, and the nimble footman, Tom, sprang into action. "Yes, Your Grace."

They descended from their seats and gently lifted the injured man into the carriage, the crimson staining his brown coat a testament to his ordeal. The urgency of their actions was heightened by the encroaching dusk.

Susan gasped in shock as Elizabeth entered the carriage, sat on the plush black leather seat, and cradled the man's head on her lap to keep his head steady from the bumpy carriage ride.

"Do not fret so much, Susan. He needs urgent help. We cannot think of propriety at a time like this."

Susan pursed her lips, her tell-tale sign of disapproval, but Elizabeth was not bothered. A man's life was at stake at the moment, and that was all that mattered.

As the carriage resumed its journey towards the dower house, she could not help but steal glances at the tall and broad-shouldered man she now held within the sanctuary of her conveyance. Moonlight filtered through the trees, casting a soft glow on his features, but she could not make out his face. The brittle air bit through the velvet lining of the carriage as the familiar silhouette of the manor rose on the horizon. Upon reaching the house, she wasted no time in summoning the housekeeper and directing the servants to prepare a chamber for their unexpected guest. She directed the men to lay him on the plush four-poster bed in the room and go fetch the doctor. She sat beside him and instructed Susan to fetch a bowl of water and a clean cloth.

As she brushed away a lock of damp hair from his forehead and the candlelight illuminated his face, a gasp escaped her lips. Recognition struck her like a bolt of lightning. The familiar lines of his square face, Grecian nose, firm lips, and clean-shaven jaw, weathered by time but etched with the same handsomeness she remembered, brought a tidal wave of emotions crashing over her. Years had painted streaks of silver through his light brown hair, making it captivating.

"Gilbert!" she murmured, her voice a mere whisper against the crackling flames of the hearth.

The owner of the name, once a forbidden figure from the corridors of her past, now lay wounded and vulnerable in her house. The revelation hit her with the force of a tempest, conjuring memories of a time when Gilbert Motley had been not just a name, but the promise of a future denied.

Years ago, her heart had beat in unison with his, and the prospect of a life together had waved before them like a fleeting dream. Yet, her parents' expectations had intervened, the appeal of a title and wealth taking precedence over young love. Memories, vivid as paint on a fresh canvas, flooded her. Stolen kisses under starlit skies, whispered dreams of a life built on love, not familial and societal expectations. But those dreams had been shattered on the altar of parental ambition. Her parents had deemed Gilbert, a mere merchant's son, unworthy of their eldest daughter. And so, with a broken heart, she had been forced to accept Edward, the future Duke of Ravenswood, as her husband.

She could not shake off the sense of injustice that still clung to her like a haunting ghost. Gilbert, a man whose worth transcended titles and wealth, had been cast aside in favour of Edward, just because of a dukedom and promise of wealth.

The wavering of the candlelight played upon Gilbert's face, and she found herself caught in a tangle of conflicting emotions. Pity flowed through her for his current plight mingled with regret for the life they might have shared—a life that now seemed lost to the relentless march of time.

"My lady!" Susan stood by the door with worry etched on her round face. "Is anything amiss? You look like you have seen a ghost."

Elizabeth smiled sadly, pulling a loose strand of her blonde hair behind her ear. "A ghost from my past, Susan."

Frowning, the elderly maid covered the distance between them. She peered at the man and sighed with relief. "I thought he was dead."

Elizabeth shook her head.

"Then why do you look so sad?"

"Do you remember Gilbert?"

Susan inhaled sharply as her eyes enlarged like saucers. "You do not mean..."

Elizabeth nodded with the same sad smile. "I do not understand what fate is playing at."

"Oh, my lady. You must see to it that he leaves at once. Perhaps he should be taken into the village, and someone paid to tend to him until he recovers."

Elizabeth's face creased into a frown. "No. I shall tend to him myself."

"Surely, you do not mean that. It is not proper, especially since..." Susan drifted to a stop and bit her lip.

"Since I have a history with him?" Elizabeth concluded and laughed bitterly. "The past is the past, Susan. I shall see to it that he recovers fully and then send him on his way."

Susan gazed at her with scepticism, but nodded. Elizabeth looked away, hoping nothing untoward would happen to alter her decision and make her regret it.

The village doctor arrived a short while later and proclaimed that Gilbert was stabbed in the chest, but he would survive because the wound was not so deep, and the blade had missed his heart by mere inches. Although he lost a lot of blood, he would make a full recovery. The wound should be kept clean always to avoid an infection.

And so, in the quiet solitude of her bedchamber, with the wounded Gilbert resting under her roof, Elizabeth realised she stood at the precipice of a past she thought she had buried. She contemplated the twists of fate that had made their paths cross once more and what the future held in store for them.

Chapter Two

Dawn crept through the break in the heavy drapes, painting the floor with silvery stripes. Elizabeth barely noticed as she hunched over Gilbert. Her fingers, guided by years of dressing wounds on her adventurous son, cleaned the jagged knife wound on his chest and re-bandaged it with gentle expertise that surprised even herself. The room was steeped in quietness, interrupted only by the occasional crackle of the fireplace. Her nimble fingers moved with purpose; her gaze focused on the task at hand.

"Duchess," Susan voiced her disapproval from the corner of the room. "This is unseemly. A lady of your stature should not be tending to a commoner's wounds."

Elizabeth shot Susan a pointed look, her sky-blue eyes reflecting a determination that brooked no argument. "Kindness knows no station, Susan. This man needs our help, and I shall not turn my back on him."

"My lady," Susan drew abreast, her displeasure showing on pursed lips and furrowed brows. "Surely, Wilton or Tom could attend to him. Such unpleasant tasks are unbecoming of your station."

Elizabeth barely glanced up. "Nonsense, Susan. He needs a woman's touch, someone who remembers poultices and bandages instead of manly hands." Her voice, though firm, held a tremor that betrayed the emotional tangle of nursing the man she once loved. Susan sighed, understanding the resolute will of her mistress. She continued her silent censure but did not intervene further.

Years of duty and decorum had sculpted Elizabeth into a duchess, but beneath the veneer of propriety, she was still the young woman who had given her heart to the merchant's son. A sigh left her lips, a mournful reverberation of lost dreams.

As she carefully tended to the wound, memories long confined to the recesses of her heart resurfaced like ghosts from the past. The touch of her fingers on Gilbert's skin stirred recollections of a time when love had blossomed, unburdened by the weight of societal beliefs.

She pondered again on the providence that brought him back into her life. Was he on his way to her manor when he got waylaid? Had he heard she lost her husband years ago and all her children were now wed and then sought her? Over the past few hours, as she sat by his bedside, she had conjured different scenarios as to the reason he was now lying in bed in her house. Such thoughts brought back fond memories of their time together.

"He was to be my husband," Elizabeth confessed in a hushed tone, her gaze fixed on the task at hand. "Many years ago, when I was but a debutante."

Susan's eyes widened in surprise, and she settled into a chair, eager to hear the tale that had been cloaked in the mist of secrecy when she was newly employed as Elizabeth's maid.

"I never really knew much about you and the man called Gilbert, whom your mother forbade me to ever mention in the manor. All I knew from the gossip of the other servants was that a man almost led you astray. Moreover, you did not want to talk about him when I asked."

Elizabeth smiled reflectively. "Because the pain had been too much to bear." Her mother had sacked her personal maid who hid her whereabouts from her parents whenever she snuck out to meet Gilbert. She had hired an elderly lady companion, Susan, with strict instructions never to let her out of her sight. Susan had done her job excellently.

"What happened?" Susan asked tentatively.

"My parents, driven by the glamour of titles and wealth, denied our love," Elizabeth continued, her voice carrying regret. "They insisted I marry Edward because he would someday become a duke and me, a duchess. Gilbert had no title, and his family lacked the wealth deemed necessary for a match of our standing."

As she spoke, her mind drifted back to a time when stolen moments with Gilbert were the essence of her clandestine happiness. "I used to sneak out, a lot," she admitted. "I would slip away from the suffocating walls of my parents' house just to meet him. Riding through the moonlit countryside, fishing by the serene lakes, and hunting in the secluded woods—those were the highpoints of our love."

Tears welled in her eyes, unshed droplets that reflected the glistening memories of a time when their hearts beat as one. "I loved him," she whispered. "I loved him so much, but it was all for naught."

"I am so sorry, my lady." Susan's face was laced with sorrow.

"We were so young then," she murmured, more to herself than her maid. "We were carefree and felt the world was at our feet." Her oval face softened into a smile. "He would be waiting for me by the oak tree with a shy smile and a basket of ripe berries. We would steal away on horseback, our joyous laughter carried on the wind as we raced through the meadows."

Her eyes, shimmering with unshed tears, drifted back to Gilbert's pale face. The years had chiselled lines around his mouth, softened by the faint ghost of that familiar, endearing smile.

"We would fish for hours on end by the stream, sharing our catches and delighting in each other's presence. And nights..." She closed her eyes, the moonlit memory gleaming behind her eyelids. "Nights filled with fireflies and promises spoken under a canopy of stars."

An unexpected sob burst from her throat, choked and raw. "I loved him so much. More than diamonds and dukes, more than propriety and family name. Even more than life itself, but my parents..."

Biting her pouting pink lip, she swallowed the bitterness that rose in her throat. The ultimatum had been cold and unforgiving. It was either she married Edward or faced social ostracising, which would affect the family.

"I had been willing to leave it all and run away with Gilbert, but when I realised what the scandal would do to my sisters, who were yet unwed, I had a rethink," she muttered with sorrow. "Being a marquess's daughter afforded us the opportunity to marry higher than our station, but not to marry for love."

With a broken heart, she had chosen duty over love, marrying Edward and burying her dreams as deep as the well. Yet even the years could not completely extinguish the embers of her first love. They flickered, hidden but alive, whenever a certain melody played, or the scent of autumn leaves touched the air.

Now, those embers roared back to life with the return of the man who had ignited them. Every time she looked at him sent shivers down her spine, kindling a storm of emotions— guilt, fear, and a yearning so fierce it threatened to shatter the dam built on years of suppressed desires.

Susan, bless her ever-understanding heart, placed a calming hand on her shoulder. "I understand, my lady," she murmured, her voice soft as velvet. "He was the one you always called 'your sunshine,' was he not?"

Elizabeth's lips curved into a sad smile. "He was. Because he chased away the shadows and filled my life with light."

Susan, her eyes softened with empathy, spoke gently. "And now, my lady?"

Tears, finally escaping the dams of her resolve, spilled down Elizabeth's cheeks. "And now, Susan, he is back. Wounded and in need. Fate, it seems, has a warped sense of humour." She sniffed and shook her head. "I do not want to talk about it anymore because the memories bring with them so much pain and regret."

"I understand. I shall tell Cook to prepare some chicken broth." Susan rose quietly and left the room.

As sunlight streamed into the chambers, Elizabeth continued to watch over Gilbert, each touch of her hand a silent prayer for the healing of more than just flesh and bone. She nursed not only his physical wounds, but the wounds of a heart that had once known the bittersweet taste of forbidden love.

Chapter Three

"I pray his fever breaks soon," Elizabeth said with immense hope as she placed the cool cloth on Gilbert's scalding forehead. The air hung heavy with the scent of herbal remedies and the traces of autumn outside the windows.

"I am sure it will, my lady. Doctor Wilber reckons it might happen later today or possibly tomorrow," Susan mentioned with a worried frown for her mistress. "My lady, I think you should get some rest. You have been at his bedside for the past three days. I fear you might fall ill from exhaustion soon."

Elizabeth smiled tiredly at her. "Then you will nurse me back to health."

"Please do not jest. I shall sit with him while you go and get some sleep," Susan suggested. "As soon as his condition changes, I shall send word to you post-haste."

Elizabeth sighed. She had maintained a constant vigil by Gilbert's bedside, her nights spent pacing the floor and praying. Each rasping breath he drew was a victory, each moment of unconsciousness a fear that he might never regain consciousness.

"Please get me a meal and then I shall go to bed for a few hours," she informed her maid.

Susan beamed with joy and hurried to do her bidding. Elizabeth's hands moved with practiced grace, swabbing Gilbert's fevered brow with the damp cloth. The fever raged within him, a storm threatening to consume his weakened form. The haunting images of highwaymen and a dagger's cruel touch resounded in the delirious mutterings that escaped his parched lips in his battle for survival.

In the quietude of the room, she knelt by the bed, a silent supplicant in a desperate plea for his survival. Her whispered prayers carried the memory of a past that refused to stay buried.

Susan returned with a hearty meal, and Elizabeth partook of it before she went to bed. After catching a few hours' sleep, she returned to her station, much to Susan's displeasure. However, the maid did not object and quietly left the room.

Elizabeth carried on attending to Gilbert in her quest to make him comfortable as he fought for his life. A sudden change in the room's atmosphere snapped her attention to his still form. He groaned and his eyes fluttered open. He blinked rapidly and stared unseeingly at her for minutes on end while she smiled at him with pent-up relief. Unexpectedly, a jolt of surprise flashed across his face. The first flicker of recognition in his eyes sent a bolt of delight through her, almost knocking her to her knees. His honey-brown eyes, though riddled with fatigue, still held the same captivating glint. A jolt of electricity, dormant for decades, sparked between them as their gazes met, sending a tremor through her heart.

Recollections, vivid as a portrait, flooded back again. Stolen kisses under starlit skies, long-winding conversations, and whispered dreams of a life built on love, not familial and societal expectations.

She found it hard to believe she was staring into the eyes of the man who could have been her everything, the man she had loved with the fiery passion of youth, the man who now lay injured and helpless like a ghost of their past risen from the ashes of time.

"Elizabeth," his raspy voice broke into her thoughts. "Is it... is it truly you, my long-lost love?"

Joy filled her heart at his words. His long-lost love? Was it possible he still felt the same way about her after so many years? Her lips trembled, unsure of what to say, what to reveal. Could she, after all these years, after a lifetime of duty and propriety, even contemplate the possi-

DAISY LANDISH

bility of rekindling a flame long extinguished? He could even be married, for all she knew.

The weight of her family's name, the whispers that would follow, and the scandal that would erupt all threatened to drown the tiny spark of hope flickering within her. But as she met his gaze, his hand seeking hers with a hesitant touch, she knew it was not just a chance encounter with a wounded stranger. Providence had a plan for them.

The firelight reflected in the tears stinging her eyes. With a voice trembling like a leaf in the wind, she whispered, "It is I, Gilbert. It is truly me."

"Where am I?" he asked hoarsely.

"You are at my dower house in Brampton," she replied quietly. "Highwaymen attacked you, and we brought you here." She smiled warmly. "I cannot tell you how relieved that you are awake at last."

He closed his eyes again and drifted off. Elizabeth was not troubled, for she knew that the worst had passed. In the hours that passed, he kept drifting in and out of his slumber, sweating profusely while she tried to keep him cool.

As the night wore on, the fevered haze that had clouded him began to dissipate. He opened his eyes wide the following morning with no hint of dazedness in them. He was finally on the road to recovery. Wincing, he lifted his head from the pillows and pushed himself into a sitting position with her help. His eyes roamed the room.

Unexpectedly, his gaze lingered on her, not with warmth, but with a chilling scrutiny. A shiver shot through her at the iciness. An unreadable expression passed over his features, and he recoiled from her proximity.

"Elizabeth," he called coldly.

The name on his lips, stripped of its familiar endearment, felt like a whip across her heart. "Yes, Gilbert," she whispered, her voice trembling with emotions she could barely control.

His eyes, sharp and icy, locked onto hers. "What are you doing here?" he asked, his voice devoid of any warmth she remembered.

"Taking care of you," she replied tightly, "just like I would anyone in need."

A bitter laugh fell from his lips. "Anyone except the man you left to bleed dry, would you not say?"

The sting of his words was a cold blade twisting in her heart. Yet, she held her ground, refusing to be bothered by his bitterness.

"Why did you really help me?" he asked, his tone laced with suspicion.

She sighed, her eyes reflecting the years of regret ensconced upon her heart. "Because no matter our history, I cannot abandon a soul in need."

The silence lengthened with unspoken words and the palpable tension of a reunion fraught with unresolved emotions. Finally, he spoke, his voice heavy with resentment. "Do you expect gratitude? A debt repaid for a kindness given?"

Her brows wrinkled, and she met his gaze unflinchingly. "I expect nothing, Gilbert. My actions are guided by humanity, not by expectations."

He shifted uncomfortably on the bed, his eyes avoiding hers. "Humanity," he muttered. "Do you even know the meaning of the word?"

"Maybe I do not," she replied calmly. She refused to rise to the bait of arguing with him about their past. It was understandable for him to be upset with her, but she did not think he would carry on with the resentment after so many years.

"You were attacked," she said with a firm voice as she changed the topic. "Can you remember what happened?"

He looked at her for minutes on end before shrugging and wincing and then looking away. Slowly, he recounted the harrowing tale of the ambush on the lonely road, the highwaymen springing from the shadows in the darkened thicket, and the sting of steel meeting flesh. When confronted by the demand for his possessions, he, fuelled by a tenacity both brave and foolhardy, had chosen defiance.

"They wanted my purse," he said, his eyes burning with annoyance. "But I would not give it to them. Not without a fight."

The audacity of the statement, of risking his life over a few coins, sparked anger in her. "A reckless fight!" she retorted. "One that could have cost you your life."

His gaze snapped to hers, the anger in their honey-brown depths mirroring her own. "And what difference would that have made to you? After all, leaving me was not exactly sparing my life, was it?"

The barb struck home, the guilt that had simmered beneath the surface erupting like a spout. But beneath the pain, a stubborn resistance hardened in her. "We made choices, Gilbert," she said, her voice low but unwavering. "I made mine, and you made yours. What is past is past."

"Easy for you to say," he sneered, "from your life of jewels and titles."

The bitterness in his voice felt like icy rain against her exposed skin. The image of Edward, aloof and distant, flashed in her mind, a stark contrast to the fiery passion that had been in Gilbert's eyes in his youth and was still there, even behind the veil of anger.

She rose fluidly, her movement driven by a sudden, fierce resolve. "Perhaps," she said, her voice ringing with clarity. "But I maintain my stand. You, sir, are fortunate to be alive. Such obstinacy in the face of danger is nothing short of recklessness!"

A veil of cold detachment descended upon him as he spoke, his words laced with animosity. "I have faced danger before, *Your Grace.*" He said the title as if it were an insult. "I fought for what I believed in, even when *you* chose to forsake love for the sake of titles and wealth."

Elizabeth's jaw tightened at the accusation, but again, she refused to let his hostility breach the walls she had meticulously erected around her heart. Once more, she deigned to foist peace between them. "Gilbert, surely you must know that the past is a collection of choices and consequences," she replied evenly. "I cannot undo what has been done, but I can choose to act with kindness and decency."

"Kindness and decency?" He snorted. "Please spare me the lectures, Your Grace. We both know when you married your duke twenty-six years ago, it had nothing to do with those things."

She would not allow him to speak to her with such animosity and anger, not when she saved his life. Not when he knew nothing about her miserable marriage. Not when he was not aware that she had been locked in her room for days to avoid her sneaking out until she was taken to London like a piece of property to meet and wed Edward. "As soon as you recover, you are free to leave."

His jaw clenched, the muscles working overtime beneath his cheek. "I shall do that right away." With a grunt of effort, he climbed down from the bed, but his legs buckled, sending him crashing back onto the floor.

A scream ripped from Elizabeth's throat, a primal cry of terror and concern. She rushed to his side, cradling his head in her hands, fear momentarily eclipsing the emotions simmering beneath the surface.

"Gilbert, you stubborn man! You are still as obstinate as ever," she chided.

"If I were indeed a stubborn man, I would never have allowed you to leave me," he whispered tightly as their eyes met and held.

For a fleeting moment, the anger and acrimony seemed to melt away, replaced by a raw vulnerability. And at that moment, the unspoken words of their past hung heavy in the air. Would they rebuild the bridge, risking scandal and societal censure, or turn away, forever clinging to the ghosts of what could have been?

Unconsciousness claimed him once more. A surge of panic and concern gripped Elizabeth's heart as she witnessed his weakened state. Her initial resolve wavered, and she could not deny the spring of emotions that surged within her. Had she really done the right thing in not taking Susan's advice and not allowing someone else to nurse him back to health in the village? His hostility had come as a surprise. Perhaps when he woke up again, she would send Wilton and Tom to find a carer for him so she could be free from all the memories of the past. Could she ever be free, especially now that they had been resurrected by his presence?

Chapter Four

Hours crawled by, each tick of the grandfather clock stretching Elizabeth's already frayed nerves. Susan bustled about, making calming pronouncements and hot tea, but her concern was palpable. The room held a hushed tension as Elizabeth, her eyes displaying concern, kept a watchful gaze on Gilbert's still form.

"He will be all right, my lady," Susan soothed, patting her shoulder. "The fever has broken, and his breathing is steady. He is strong, and your care has already worked wonders."

Elizabeth nodded, though the worry marking her features persisted. She could not forget the words he had spoken before he fell unconscious again. Her own hasty words uttered in anger and self-defence, troubled her conscience. Perhaps she should not have pushed him away and reacted to his blatant animosity. After all, his bitterness reflected hers.

"I should never have asked him to leave, which made him rise from the bed and become unconscious." She chewed on her bottom lip as she stared at Gilbert's pale face.

"You meant when he recovered. Please do not blame yourself for his stubbornness," Susan pointed out before she drifted out of the room to fetch her a meal.

Elizabeth observed her charge and shook her head. She wished she had not met him again because of the constant flailing emotions running through her. Why would life be so cruel to her to remind her of what she had lost?

Hours passed like the gentle drift of autumn leaves, and then, as if responding to the unspoken yearnings of her heart, Gilbert's eyes flapped open. The grogginess of the fever was completely lifted in their depths.

"Gilbert," Elizabeth greeted, her voice a blend of relief and coolness.

He attempted to rise but winced, the pain from the effects of his encounter with the highwaymen evident.

"You must lie still," she advised.

He shook his head. "I must apologise, Your Grace, for the way I spoke to you earlier. My gratitude to you for saving my life knows no bounds."

Elizabeth, her heart softened by his genuine apology, inclined her head gracefully. The vulnerability in his eyes, raw and unguarded, tugged at her heartstrings. "Apology accepted. There is no need for such formalities. Elizabeth will do."

He nodded and grimaced. His hand, warm and roughened by years of toil, found hers, a lifeline thrown across the abyss of their past. The touch, familiar yet different, sent a thrill of electricity through her veins.

Susan entered the room just then, and Elizabeth jerked back her hand and rose, her face flushed.

"Susan, Gil... er ... Mr Motley is finally awake. Please see to it that his wound is re-bandaged, and he is well fed." She turned to the injured man. "Please excuse me."

Lifting the skirts of her yellow muslin gown, she exited the room with swift steps and hurried out of the manor to her garden; a place where she usually found respite. But nothing, not even the fragrance of dried leaves or the coolness of the autumn breeze, could calm the turmoil within her.

Why did I allow him to touch me? Surely, he must have felt the tremor that ran through my body. He must think I have pined for him all these years.

Embarrassment caused her cheeks to redden, and she made a resolve to stay away from him. She could only hope that his recovery would be fast, and that he would be on his way soon enough.

Despite her resolution, Elizabeth could not help going to his bedchamber a few hours later. She found him asleep and stayed by his bedside for a moment, observing him and remembering the times they had laid in the fields under the moonlit and star-studded sky.

Days passed and Gilbert was recovering slowly. Elizabeth's curiosity got the better of her one morning as she pondered on the life he had lived after she was forced to marry Edward.

"Tell me, Gilbert," she began, her gaze thoughtful, "what has life dealt you since our paths diverged?"

He sighed. "Life, my lady, has been a journey of unforeseen turns. After you...you... chose another path, I faced hardships and trials, yet I persevered. I became a husband, a father, and a widower."

The vulnerability in his words resonated with her, stirring compassion that bridged the chasm of years. "You are a widower?" she inquired gently.

He nodded, a melancholic shadow passing over his features. "Yes, my wife passed away many years ago. My only son is now married with a family of his own in Cornwall."

Years peeled away as they shared snippets of their lives after their relationship came to an abrupt end. He spoke of a life dedicated to trade, the satisfaction of building from the ground up, yet a loneliness that reflected the hollowness in her own heart. As they spoke, the barriers erected by time began to crumble as they slowly and hesitantly reconnected.

"And what brought you to these parts?" she asked, her curiosity piqued.

"I was on my way to visit a friend when those highwaymen decided to make their untimely appearance."

A wry smile tugged at her lips. "It seems fate had other plans for your journey."

"Indeed. An old uncle warned me to be careful as the incidents of highwaymen had risen in these parts, but I did not listen."

She frowned. "An old uncle?"

He nodded and said, "The Duke of Chesterton. We are related from my late mother's side of the family."

The revelation that he was a distant relative to Amelia's husband,

Jonathan, the Marquess of Bilcester, brought a wry smile to her lips. A twist of fate, indeed, that she would find a family connection in the man who once held her heart. But she did not voice it.

He, in turn, listened with rapt attention as she spoke of her children, their lives blossoming with love and new families. His guarded gaze lingered on hers when she mentioned Edward.

And then, amidst the gentle flow of their conversation, the question that hung heavy in the air finally tumbled out. "Are you saying you are now a widow?"

She took a deep breath and let it out slowly. "Yes, Gilbert," she said, her voice gaining strength with each word. "I am a widow."

And you are a widower.

The unspoken words hung heavy in the space between them, a truth laid bare, and a spark of possibility arising between them.

As dusk fell, painting the room in a palette of soft rose and amber, Elizabeth gazed at Gilbert's face, his handsome features softened by sleep.

The man before her was not the carefree youth who had captured her heart years ago, but a man sculpted by time and trials. And she was no longer the young girl bound by societal chains, but a woman who had faced an unhappy marriage and emerged wiser. Her heart stirred by the whispers of a second chance beat a rapid thud against her chest.

Could they reignite their past love?

Chapter Five

A few days later, Elizabeth, spoon poised over the soup bowl, observed Gilbert, her heart a tangled nest of conflicting emotions. He was still pale and weak from his blood loss and fever, but the shadow of death that had lurked in his eyes was gone. His recovery had progressed steadily.

As she attended to him, she could not ignore the gentle stirrings of feelings long kept at bay. A familiar warmth budded within her, and she could not ignore the undeniable truth. Her heart, against all rationality, longed for the man lying before her.

The years might have marked lines around his eyes and turned some strands of his hair grey, but beneath the surface, she recognised the man who had once held the entirety of her heart in his calloused hands. Again, every memory came flooding back; the moonlit dances, their laughter echoing through meadows and just basking in each other's company.

But reality cast a long shadow over their reawakened connection. She was Elizabeth Norrington, the Dowager Duchess of Ravenswood, bound by the shackles of propriety and a family name older than time. He was Gilbert Motley, a merchant by trade, a distant relative of nobility, yet still as far removed from her world as the stars from the earth.

The whispers, the scandal, the ostracising...the mere thought of it sent a shiver down her spine. Her children settled in their own nests of love and respectability, would not understand, particularly as she had drummed family duty into their ears countless times. Society would be merciless, their tongues dripping venom as they dissected her every move, her every glance. No one would understand such love between them if they ever decided to give in to it again.

As she spooned the broth into Gilbert's mouth, his hand brushing hers in a fleeting touch, the fire of possibility refused to be extinguished. It was a forbidden flame, wavering at the edges of her carefully planned life, threatening to burn down the walls she had built around her heart.

"Are you all right, my lady?" Gilbert's quietly spoken question jolted her from her tangled thoughts. "Is anything amiss?"

Smiling softly, she replied, "Not at all."

He peered at her keenly. "Are you tired of taking care of me? I could be on my way in a matter of hours if that is what you want."

She hastily shook her head. "Not at all, Gilbert. I was merely lost in thoughts."

"Lost in thoughts?" He frowned. "Is anything amiss? I mean, with your children."

His obvious concern warmed her heart. "No. They are fine. Please excuse me." She got up elegantly, thrust the half-eaten bowl of food into his hands, and hastily left the room, feeling his eyes boring into her back. She feared if she stayed there any longer, she would blurt her concerns to him. It would be an embarrassing conversation, given that she did not know if he still felt the same way about her. That he enjoyed her company was no basis for her to think that there was more to it.

She hurried to her drawing room and paced, her footsteps soundless on the thick carpet. The door opened, and a worried-looking Susan entered.

"My lady, are you alright?"

She whirled around and stared at the older woman. How could she make her understand the chaos raging inside her?

Susan observed her with a discerning eye, her concern evident in the creasing of her brows. "This has something to do with your guest, does it not?"

Elizabeth gasped. "How did you know?"

"My lady," she ventured, her voice filled with gentle concern, "you have been spending a considerable amount of time with him. Are you sure it is wise?"

Elizabeth sighed. "I cannot deny the feelings that have resurfaced, Susan. But I fear society's censure. I am a dowager duchess, and he—a commoner. Such an alliance would be met with scandal."

Susan drew abreast and placed a reassuring hand on her shoulder. "Feelings are not bound by societal expectations. If your heart calls for his company, perhaps there is a path to tread that avoids scandal."

Elizabeth shook her head. "I have worked hard to uphold the family name, to ensure my children's happiness and secure their places in society. I cannot risk tarnishing that legacy."

"Love is a force beyond our control," Susan remarked. "Perhaps it is time to consider your own happiness."

Elizabeth sighed and continued pacing the floor. "I do not know if I can do that." Suddenly, a smile curved the corners of her lips. "He makes me remember, Susan," she confessed, her voice soft. "Not just the pain of those lost years, but the joy, the laughter, the... love."

Susan smiled wistfully. "I understand. You were not a duchess then, just Elizabeth, a girl with a big heart and a head full of dreams."

But she was a dowager duchess now, Elizabeth reminded herself, the weight of responsibility settling like a heavy cloak. "He is a commoner," she repeated as if saying it constantly would change his status. "My children are married, their lives built on the foundation of titles and lineage. Can I do this to them? Risk bringing shame to their doorstep? Especially after I never stopped telling them to marry for duty's sake even when love came knocking."

"Shame? Or are you speaking of fear? Fear of what Society might say, what your children might think, what you might believe?"

Her words struck a chord, a deep, resonant note that vibrated through the layers of Elizabeth's self-doubt. Was it shame she felt, or the echo of societal bounds she had not yet broken? Was it her children she worried about, or the uncertainty of a life with Gilbert?

She closed her eyes and looked inward. She had a lot of thinking to do and a decision to make.

The following days found Elizabeth caught in internal turmoil. She continued her ministrations to Gilbert, tending to his needs with a grace that belied the tumult within. Each bandage changed, every spoonful of meals fed, and each moment spent in his company deepened the emotional the attachment she felt for him.

One evening, as the sun dipped below the horizon, she sought solace in the garden. Susan joined her, their footsteps punctuating the quiet embrace of nature.

"Still conflicted, my lady?" Susan inquired gently.

Elizabeth nodded, her gaze fixed on the changing hues of the autumn landscape. "I fear the condemnations of society, Susan. They are unforgiving, and I cannot bear to bring scandal upon my family. I have seen it happen time and time again, and I will not do that to them. Charlotte narrowly escaped a horrific scandal, and I do not intend to bring back the memory when my name is tied to one. Amelia's courtship with Jonathan also caused tongues to wag. William falling in love with Sarah and not his betrothed almost caused a scandal. Finding Sophia alone with Stephen at a secluded spot almost gave me apoplexy. I tried my best to make sure that my children were scandal free and that the Norrington name and Ravenswood title were protected at all costs. All my life, possibly because my mother also drummed it into me about the dangers of being talked about by the *ton*, I have been wary of scandals. I cannot cause one now."

Susan responded calmly. "You have done well as both a duchess and dowager duchess, but it is time for you to think about yourself. There is no shame in acknowledging your feelings. Mr Motley holds a place in your heart, and that is a truth you cannot deny. Society may judge, but your happiness is equally paramount. The fickle *ton* will always talk, but it will blow over as usual and they will find someone else to talk about."

"Perhaps you are right. But the consequences of pursuing this path are daunting. A dowager duchess and a commoner. It is a union that would invite censure and end up bringing unhappiness between Gilbert and me."

Susan shook her head. "I do not think so. Besides, you both desire to travel. The elites will be forgotten during your many trips around the world. Why, I cannot tell you how happy I am that you will not embark on your trip alone next year. Fate has provided you with a companion to make the journey more exhilarating."

As they strolled through the garden, Elizabeth wrestled with her emotions, torn between the duty she felt towards her family and the yearnings of her own heart. The choices she made in the days to come would determine not only her own fate but the delicate balance of the family name she had so diligently safeguarded.

Chapter Six

"This is beautiful," Elizabeth said at the sight of the undulating landscape ahead.

Gilbert chuckled. "Not as beautiful as you."

She laughed softly. "Even after four children? I will have you know that I have three grandchildren with more on the way."

His eyes held a warmth that left her breathless. "Even if you become a great-grandmother, old and wrinkled, you will remain the most beautiful woman in the world to me."

She hastily looked away. Sweet Mary, she could not believe that she was blushing like a shy schoolgirl at her age. Gilbert's compliments still made her feel special.

Astride her trusty mare with her shiny blonde tresses whipping in the wind, Elizabeth felt a familiar thrill course through her veins. Beside her, Gilbert, atop his sleek stallion, grinned, his eyes sparkling with the same mischievous joy she had not witnessed in years.

The brown and yellow leaves made crunching noises as they leisurely rode their horses along the tree-lined path. The air was crisp, carrying the promise of a golden afternoon bathed in sunlight. As Gilbert's strength returned, so did the memories of their past, drawing them together with awakened emotions.

They were at the edge of the estate, preparing for an impromptu horse race, the thrill of thundering hooves and wind rushing through their hair reminiscent of days long past.

"Are you sure you are fit for a race?" she asked him with a twinkle in her eyes, brushing lint from her dark blue riding habit.

His brows curved. "Is that an excuse to get out of the race?"

She laughed heartily. "I hope you will take your defeat gracefully."

He grinned. "We shall see."

The spirited horses, vibrant with energy, carried them across the sprawling fields, laughter and joyous banter resounding in the open air. It was a reckless, exhilarating freedom, a taste of the stolen moments that had fuelled their clandestine love years ago.

Elizabeth, her cheeks flushed with exhilaration, crossed the designated finish line first and reined in her horse as they reached the edge of the woods. Gilbert, his gaze bright with mirth, pulled up beside her. "You have not lost your touch, my lady," he remarked, a glimmer in his eyes.

"And you remain a formidable opponent," she replied, a playful glint in her gaze. The camaraderie they shared in those carefree moments brought them closer.

Later, beneath the shade of a towering oak, still flushed from the chase, they spread a picnic blanket, remnants of childhood games scattered around them. They devoured cheese and crusty bread, shared juicy apples, and laughed over silly card games; the air thick with the sweet scent of fallen leaves.

Their escapades continued into the realm of the hunting grounds, where the rustle of leaves served as a prelude to the chase. The thrill of the hunt, the shared glances that spoke volumes, transported them back to a time when the world was their playground, and societal obligations held no sway.

In the evenings, they retreated to the cosy confines of Elizabeth's dower house, where card games unfolded against the backdrop of candlelight. The competitive banter flowed effortlessly, reminiscent of their glorious past.

One afternoon, as they strolled by the serene pond where swans swam elegantly upon the water, a quiet settled upon them. Elizabeth, feeding the graceful birds, finally broke the silence. With her heart swelling with emotions that defied the passage of time, she turned to Gilbert.

"Gilbert," she began, "we have skirted around the shadows of our past for too long. I believe it is time we confront them."

He met her gaze steadily. "What do you really want us to talk about?"

She took a deep breath, her focus fixed on the rippling water. "Our past, Gilbert. The time when our hearts beat in unison, when we shared sweet moments that my family and society tried to keep from us."

A solemn silence hung between them before he spoke. "I remember those days, Elizabeth. Days filled with laughter and love. But they were overshadowed by the pain of losing you."

She turned to face him, a vulnerability in her eyes that mirrored his own. "My parents discovered our secret. They forbade me from ever seeing you again. When I tried to sneak out of the house to reach out to you about their discovery, they caught me and locked me away before spiriting me off to London, where I was compelled to marry Edward."

Gilbert's eyes widened, surprise playing across his face. "I thought... I thought you had played with my affections. It broke my heart to hear about your marriage, and I convinced myself you had never truly cared for me. That you had merely toyed with my feelings out of boredom until you got married."

The accusation, unspoken for so long, ripped through her like a blade. Tears spilled down her cheeks, her heart aching for how he must have felt; heartbroken and betrayed. She reached out, her hand cupping his, a silent apology for the stolen years, the unfulfilled promises. "That was never the case. I loved you with every beat of my heart. The pain I felt, being torn away from you, haunted me through the years."

He engulfed her hand in his, his calloused fingers brushing against her delicate skin. "I thought... I thought you..." he choked, his eyes blazing with pain. "I thought the very wrong things about you. Your marriage made me feel like a discarded, withered flower."

"Never," she whispered. "Never, Gilbert. My heart was yours, and yours alone. My parents..." she closed her eyes, the bitterness rising in her throat. "My parents saw our love as a threat, a stain on their precious lineage."

She poured out the story. The ultimatum her mother gave her, her need to put her sisters first, the suffocating air of her London season, and the miserable marriage to Edward, a man she had never loved and who had loved drinking and gambling causing their family to be thrust into penury. Her only joy was her children.

He pulled her into a comforting embrace, the burden of years lifting in that tender moment. Elizabeth, her voice choked with emotion, whispered against his shoulder, "I am so sorry for what you must have endured. It was not a choice I made willingly."

"And I am so sorry for hating you all these years, thinking you did not deem me worthy of being your husband. I am also sorry for your forced marriage. I wish there was something I could have done to stop it. And your misery all these years."

As silence descended, the only sound the gentle lapping of the water and the swishing of leaves, he pulled her closer, his embrace a haven against the storms of their past. His warm breath mingled with hers, his soothing whispers a balm to her soul. Tears continued to fall unheeded down her face.

"It is all right, my beauty," he murmured, his voice thick with emotion. "We are here now. Together."

In that embrace, by the tranquil pond, under the watchful gaze of the swans, their past and present merged, finding solace in their renewed association.

As the sun dipped low, forming a warm radiance over the pond and the swans slithering upon its surface, Elizabeth and Gilbert found succour in their past riddled with heartache.

Chapter Seven

"You are positively glowing, my lady," Susan remarked, her hands skilfully arranging the delicate strands of Elizabeth's blonde hair as she helped her prepare for dinner.

A soft smile touched Elizabeth's lips. "It appears the autumn winds have stirred something within me, Susan."

Susan beamed. "It does the heart good to see."

Elizabeth blushed. "It has been... a while," she admitted. "Since I felt this... alive."

"All thanks to Mr Motley, no doubt."

Elizabeth met Susan's gaze in the mirror, and a sigh escaped her. "Yes, Susan. It seems that my heart has found its way back to him. I love him. I think I never stopped," she confessed.

Susan's eyes sparkled with joy, her hands momentarily stilling their work. "Oh, my lady! This is wonderful news! Perhaps fate has granted you a second chance at love."

Elizabeth shook her head, a touch of sadness in her eyes. "You know as well as I do that such sentiments are luxuries society rarely affords. Gilbert will be leaving tomorrow, and I cannot—"

Susan interrupted; her voice filled with optimism. "But if you love him and he loves you, is it not worth the risk? Forget about the family name and societal expectations—sometimes, we must follow our hearts."

Elizabeth shook her head. "It is a fool's dream. A scandal waiting to happen. My children, Society..."

She trailed off. How could she, who had advised her children to prioritize duty above all else, now seek happiness at the expense of their reputation? The whispers, the shunning, the shame... it was a future too terrible to contemplate.

Elizabeth looked at herself in the mirror, a conflicted expression marring her features. "I spent a lifetime advising my children to marry for duty, for the family name, and I made sure they did. How can I now set aside those principles for my own desires?"

She rose gracefully and walked towards the door. The skirts of her orchid blue silk dress with white lace trimmings showed off her slightly curvy figure.

As they descended the grand staircase to the dining room, Elizabeth's heart twisted at how handsome Gilbert looked in his black evening clothes as he waited by the door.

"You look as beautiful as ever, Elizabeth," he said with a dazzling smile before taking her hand.

"Thank you, Gilbert," she replied, flushed as he led her into the large dining room.

The dinner that followed was a lively affair, filled with laughter and memories. The table was adorned with fine silverware and crystal glasses and platters of roasted pheasant and spiced potatoes and rich gravy.

After dinner, they walked through the moonlit garden. Gilbert, his eyes tender, broke the silence. "Elizabeth, my love, the past days with you have been like a dream. I cannot bear the thought of leaving you behind."

Elizabeth's gaze drifted to the moonlit path ahead, a veil of melancholy clouding her eyes. "Gilbert, we must face reality. Society will not allow us to be together. I have already had my chance at love, and I cannot jeopardize the family name for a fleeting romance."

Gilbert took her hand, his grip gentle yet pleading. "But Elizabeth, we can find a way. Love has a power of its own—"

She withdrew her hand, and a tear rolled down her face, glistening in the moonlight. "I have given my children advice I should now follow myself. Duty and family name come before personal desires. I cannot let our emotions blind us to the consequences."

His expression a mixture of heartbreak and determination, Gilbert declared, "I love you, Elizabeth. I never stopped loving you. I would face any consequence for the chance to be with you."

Then, he stopped, his eyes burning with desperate love. "Elizabeth," he pleaded, his voice rough with emotion. "Do not let us part ways again. I love you, with every fiber of my being. Let us defy the *ton* and build a life together, no matter the cost."

But she could not bring herself to meet his gaze. His words, promises of a forbidden future, tore at her conscience. "We cannot, Gilbert," she choked out, the words tasting like ashes on her tongue. "My children..."

"Your children," he countered, his voice rising in frustration. "Would they truly turn their backs on you, on their mother, for finding happiness again? For loving a man who cherishes you as I do?"

His argument resonated, but still, the weight of expectations crushed her. "The peer of the realm will not accept it, Gilbert. They will never forgive us. We will be shunned everywhere we go and given the cut. My children will face the same fate."

And with that, she turned and fled. He called her name, but she refused to look back, running blindly through the silent gardens, carrying the echoes of his declaration and the weight of her own refusal like chains around her heart.

She reached her room and collapsed onto the chaise longue, her sobs muffled by the silk cushions.

The words Susan had spoken earlier echoed in the emptiness of her heart: "Do not let fear dictate your happiness."

How could she reconcile her longing for love with the duty she owed her family and her title?

Chapter Eight

Morning dawned over the dower house, casting a muted glow upon the estate. Elizabeth faced the new day with a heaviness in her heart. Sleep had eluded her, the spectre of impending farewells lingering in her restless dreams.

In an attempt to distract herself from the inevitable parting, she made her way to the serene pond nestled within the estate. The swans, graceful in their movements, glided across the surface, unaware of her misery.

She poured the feed into the water, watching as the swans approached with speed. A single tear showed the conflict that raged within her. Gilbert, the man she had loved and lost once before, was about to leave. Would it be forever? Were their paths destined never to merge?

As the morning sun filtered through the trees, forming dappled shadows across the estate, Gilbert, his face lined with the same sorrow that reflected her own, appeared on the path, his footsteps soft on the leaves.

"Elizabeth," he murmured, his voice thick with feelings. "Do not do this. Do not shut me out again."

His plea sliced through her like a knife, the words reverberating through the craving in her own soul. He was not just asking for a goodbye; he was asking for a future – a life imprinted in adventures across continents they had once dreamt of.

He held out his hand, his eyes shimmering with love. "Come with me, Elizabeth," he pleaded, his voice husky with emotion. "Let us build our own world, away from the stifling whispers and disapproving glances. Remember our plans, the maps we used to pore over, the atlases filled with dreams?"

Her heart, ached by years of duty and unspoken longing, yearned to break free from its cage and soar alongside him. But reality cast a long shadow. "The *ton* would not accept it, Gilbert," she whispered with tears. "The scandal... the shame... I cannot bear to bring that upon my children."

He scoffed. "Shame? For loving the man you choose? For embracing happiness after years of living in an unhappy marriage? Have you not sacrificed enough to those 'expectations' they forced upon you? Have you not already once buried your heart at their behest?"

His words struck a raw nerve, a truth she had spent years burying beneath layers of resignation. Was she repeating the same mistake, sacrificing her heart on the altar of duty, just as she had in her youth?

"Elizabeth," he spoke softly, deep emotions carried in his voice. "Remember the world we once dreamt of in our youth? We can experience all that and more if you would only put yourself first for once. You told me of your desire to travel in the coming year. We could do all that and more together."

With her gaze fixed on the swans, she sighed with a mixture of longing and resignation. She could not think of anything more satisfying than to travel the world with Gilbert by her side. "You know as well as I do that such a path is fraught with challenges. My children—"

He interrupted, a fervent plea in his eyes. "Your children are grown. They have found their paths, and it is time for you to rediscover your own happiness. Do not let the shackles of society bind you once more."

Her heart wavered, the truthfulness of his words resonating within her. For a moment, she considered the allure of a life unburdened by societal limitations. To roam the world with Gilbert, to revel in the freedom denied to her in her youth. Throwing caution to the wind, grabbing his hand, and stepping into the unknown with him. To forget the suffocating rules and the judgmental stares, and embrace the exhilarating freedom of a life chosen, a love unhidden. The prospect tugged at her heartstrings.

Remember who you are, Elizabeth. Edward's family will not take kindly to you soiling the Norrington name and Ravenswood title.

Again, duty called out to her. Duty to her family and to the title she bore. Could she risk bringing shame to their doorstep, threatening their lives built on the foundation of titles and lineage?

With a heavy sigh, she turned away from his imploring gaze. "Gilbert, as much as my heart yearns for such a life with you, I cannot forsake the responsibilities that bind me. The *ton* may be merciful, but I cannot disregard the consequences our actions would have on my family. For them, I have to stay."

He reached for her hand, his touch a gentle caress. "Elizabeth, do not repeat the mistakes of the past. Choose your happiness. Choose us."

Her eyes, pools of regret, met his. "For the sake of my children, I must make the difficult choice. I cannot embark on this journey with you."

Gilbert, a storm of emotions etched across his face, bowed his head in reluctant acceptance. "Then, my love, I bid you farewell."

He turned, his shoulders slumped in defeat, his footsteps echoing like the knell of her shattered dreams. As he walked away, leaving behind the autumn-kissed haven they had briefly shared, Elizabeth felt the heaviness of her decision settle upon her. A tear traced a solitary path down her cheek.

Returning to the dower house, she sought the seclusion of her room. The tears she had suppressed in his presence now flowed freely. The autumn romance, a fleeting interlude that had stirred dormant emotions, left in its wake a heart broken once more.

Chapter Nine

"I wish you had not come back into my life. Again, you have taken my heart with you and left me hollow," Elizabeth whispered to her reflection in the mirror.

In the solitude of her chamber, she questioned the decisions that had led to her loneliness. Once more, duty had triumphed over the pursuit of happiness. The family name, a venerable mantle she had worn with pride, now felt like a heavy shroud, concealing the longing for a love she had let slip away again.

When she was forced to marry Edward twenty-six years ago, a man she did not know much about, let alone love, she had thought she would never experience such heartbreak again. But now, it felt as if she was wallowing in misery she would never get out of.

"I made the right decision," she said, dabbing at her eyes with her perfumed dainty handkerchief. "I love my children too much to put my own happiness before theirs."

But the weeks that had passed without Gilbert felt as if she were merely existing with no purpose in life. Mayhap she should travel to Ravenswood. William and Sarah's first child was almost due. Or perhaps she could go and visit Charlotte. Her twin children, Reginald and Henrietta, were always a delight to be around. Amelia's daughter,

Annabel, also brought joy to her heart. Perhaps she would visit all her children before she embarked on her trip...alone.

A knock on the door heralded the intrusion of unexpected visitors. Startled, Elizabeth turned to find her four children—William, Charlotte, Amelia, and Sophia—standing before her. Surprise painted her features, and she rose from her dresser stool with joy and confusion coursing through her.

"My darlings! I hope all is well. You did not inform me of your intention to visit. And all together. Is anything amiss?"

They rushed forward to hug her and inform her that all was well, but they wished to discuss something with her. Still looking worried, she led them to her drawing room, where she rang for tea and biscuits. While they waited for the refreshments, she asked about her sons-in-law, her heavily pregnant daughter-in-law, and her grandchildren.

"Mother," William, the eldest, spoke with warmth after they partook of the refreshments. "We heard about Gilbert and could not stay away any longer."

Elizabeth gasped. "But how?" Then she sighed. Only one person would have told her children about her lost love. Her closest friend, Susan.

Charlotte chimed in, confirming her mother's suspicions. "Susan wrote to us, and we cannot believe you are still here, mired in solitude."

Amelia, a picture of elegance and motherhood, gently added, "Mother, it is time to put aside the mantle of duty. We have come to remind you that you deserve happiness, too."

Sophia, the youngest, rested a hand on her protruding stomach. "We have each found our happiness, Mother. It is time you find yours."

Their collective presence stirred a torrent of emotions within Elizabeth. Their eyes, filled with understanding, implored her to reconsider the choices that bound her.

"But what will people say? You all will be ostracized. He is a commoner, and I am a dowager duchess. The *ton* will tear us all to shreds," she voiced her utmost concern. "I cannot do that to you all. Not when I have been so vocal about putting duty before anything else."

"Mother," William continued, "it is okay to choose love over duty and family name. It was not until I was a man that I realised how despicable Father was, and the sacrifices you made to shield us from his wrath and flaws and make us happy. You have sacrificed enough for us, and we want to see you happy."

Elizabeth, tears pooling in her eyes, felt a mixture of gratitude and longing. Her children, once dependent on her guidance, now stood as guardians of her heart's desires. Their expressions mirrored a collective sentiment, a rallying cry for her to break free from the self-imposed shackles of societal beliefs.

Charlotte drew abreast to put her arm around her shoulders. "We have seen your sacrifices, and we are here to give you the freedom to choose love. I was heartbroken when I read how you were forced to give up the man you loved because of your family. No one deserves that. Thankfully, you have a second chance at love. Please, do not throw it away. The *ton* cannot hurt us, not if we don't allow them. Do not be afraid of a scandal. Tongues will wag, but eventually, they will also look for something else to fill their time. Your happiness with this man is all that matters."

Amelia added, "Mr Motley is the love of your life, just as we have also found our own love. Do not let him slip away again. You gave him up before because of duty. You do not have to do that again. We will all be fine."

Sophia, a glow of maternal anticipation surrounding her, spoke with an earnestness that belied her youth. "Mother, I want my child to have the example of a grandmother who chose love over convention. You have always wished to travel and now you have a companion to do it with. Do not mind what anyone says. Besides, you will be so busy exploring different continents with Mr Motley, that the *ton* would have forgotten about both of you by the time you return."

The weight of their words settled on Elizabeth's shoulders. Their message was simple: seize the chance for love, for happiness, before it slipped away like grains of sand through an open palm.

Taking a deep breath, Elizabeth wiped away the tears that had betrayed her emotions. "My dear children," she whispered, "thank you for reminding me of what truly matters. Duty may have guided my choices in the past, but love shall light the path ahead."

The room, once suffused with a sombre stillness, now resonated with a renewed sense of hope. Elizabeth, surrounded by the manifestations of her legacy, felt the tendrils of the possibility of a life of love and freedom.

As the family gathered in a warm embrace, the dower house became a sanctuary of love and understanding. With her children's support, Elizabeth decided she would embark on a journey—one that transcended duty, defied societal limitations, and embrace the promise of a second chance at love.

Chapter Ten

The journey to Gilbert's abode was one of anticipation and trepidation. Elizabeth and the ever-loyal Susan embarked on a carriage ride fraught with tension.

As the carriage traversed the winding lanes, Elizabeth's thoughts wavered between the fear of arriving too late and the craving to find Gilbert waiting, his love undiminished by the passing weeks. She prayed like she had never done before as the rolling English countryside, adorned in the warm hues of autumn, spread ahead in the distance.

Upon reaching Gilbert's residence, Elizabeth's gaze fell upon the charming facade. The stone walls exuded an ageless grace, a silent witness to the passage of time. The surrounding fields and meadows showed off a serenity that calmed her frayed nerves.

The carriage came to a gentle stop, and Elizabeth, fortified by her love, stepped onto the cobblestone pathway that led to the entrance. The air was charged with anticipation as she approached the threshold, where destiny awaited.

The sturdy wooden door swung open, revealing Gilbert, his eyes widening in astonishment and joy at the unexpected sight before him. Elizabeth, clad in a gown of lavender, held her breath, waiting for the moment to unfurl.

"Elizabeth," Gilbert breathed her name. He took a tentative step forward, as if afraid she might vanish like a mirage.

"Gilbert," she responded, her voice unsteady. "I have come... I have come because..."

He closed the distance between them, enveloping her in a tender embrace that spoke volumes. The reunion, a fusion of hearts long separated, unfolded in the quiet sanctuary of his home.

"I thought you might have set off on your travels," she confessed, her eyes seeking reassurance in his gaze.

A wistful smile played on his lips. "I could not leave without you. My heart longed for you, Elizabeth. I kept praying you would change your mind and come seek me."

Elizabeth, her emotions laid bare, took a step back to meet Gilbert's gaze directly. "Gilbert, I have spent too many years adhering to duty and societal dictates. Today, I choose love. I love you, Gilbert. I always have and I always will."

His eyes sparkled with joy. "Elizabeth, my dearest Elizabeth, I never thought this day would come. I hoped. I prayed, but the day seemed elusive. And now that it is here, I am short of words."

She laughed softly. "I, too, had been afraid to hope. The knowledge of losing you again seemed too much for me to bear. Fortunately, thanks to Susan who summoned my children to talk some sense into me, I am here to be with you forever. I will be with you until the breath ceases from my chest."

With a newfound sense of purpose, Gilbert dropped to one knee. "Will you marry me, Elizabeth? Will you be my companion in this journey of love we have been denied for so long?"

Tears of happiness rose in Elizabeth's eyes as she nodded, her heart swelling with joy. "Yes, Gilbert."

Susan, witnessing this momentous occasion, erupted into a joyous cheer, her support, and that of her children, an unspoken blessing for the union of two hearts.

In the quaint parlour of Gilbert's home, surrounded by the warmth of love and approval, Elizabeth and Gilbert embraced their destiny as they embarked on a second chance at love that promised a lifetime of sunsets and the timeless beauty of an autumn romance.

The End.
Did you enjoy *The Norrington Collection*?
Please consider rating it on Goodreads, Bookbub or your favorite retailer. Reviews help me reach new readers.

Have you read all the historical romance collections?
The Lady Series - The Allington Collection
The Lady Series - The Gillingham Collection
The Lady Series - The Blackmore Collection
The Lady Series - The Norrington Collection

Join my Newsletter for writing updates, sales, and more!
www.daisylandishromance.com

Milton Keynes UK
Ingram Content Group UK Ltd.
UKHW011833210624
444498UK00001B/95